Mighty Mighty MONSTERS

MONSTER BEACH

STONE ARCH BOOKS
a capstone imprint

Mighty Mighty Monsters are published by
Stone Arch Books, A Capstone Imprint
151 Good Counsel Drive, P.O. Box 669 Mankato,
Minnesota 56002 www.capstonepub.com

Library of Congress Cataloging-in-Publication Data
O'Reilly, Sean, 1974-
Monster beach / by Sean O'Reilly ; illustrated by Arcana Studio.
p. cm. -- (Mighty Mighty Monsters)
Summary: The Mighty Mighty Monsters make a new friend at the beach.
ISBN-13: 978-1-4342-3217-5 (library binding)
ISBN-10: 1-4342-3217-4 (library binding)
1. Graphic novels. [1. Graphic novels. 2. Monsters--Fiction. 3. Beaches--Fiction. 4. Friendship--Fiction.]
I. Arcana Studio. II. Title.
PZ7.7.O74Mm 2011
741.5'973--dc22
2011003442

Printed in the United States of America in Melrose Park, Illinois.
032011
006112LKF11

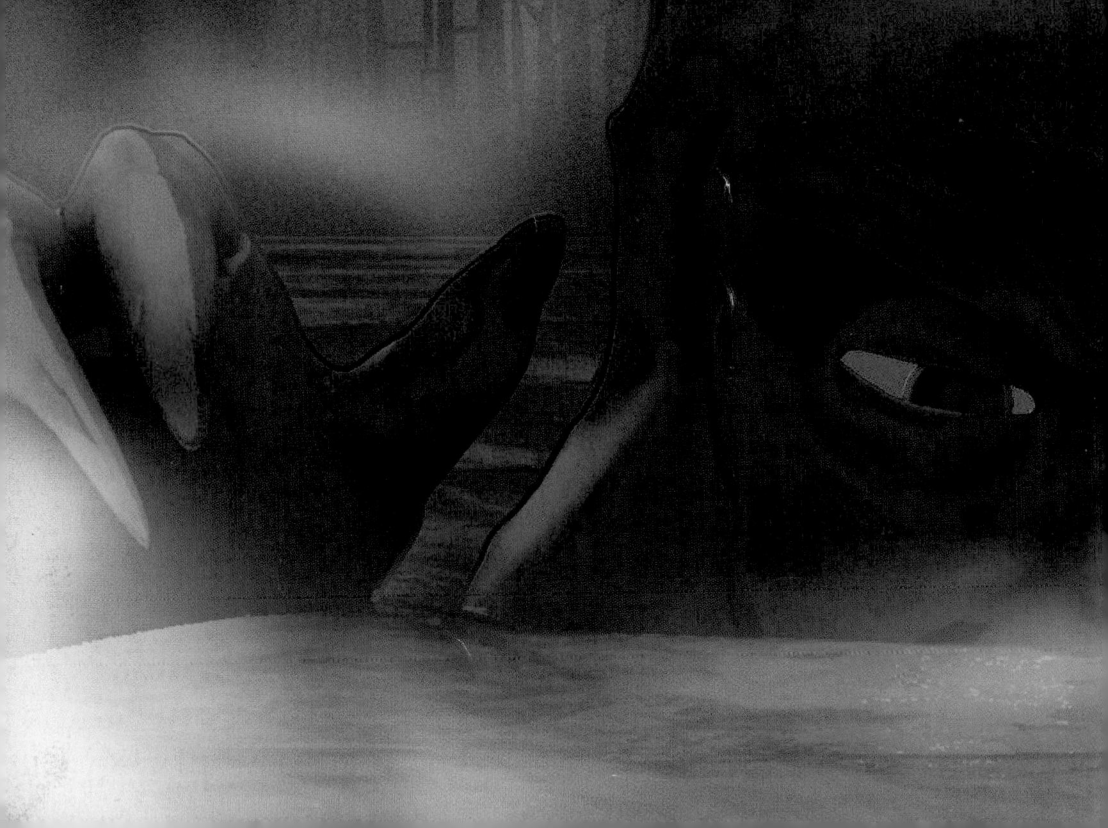

MONSTER BEACH

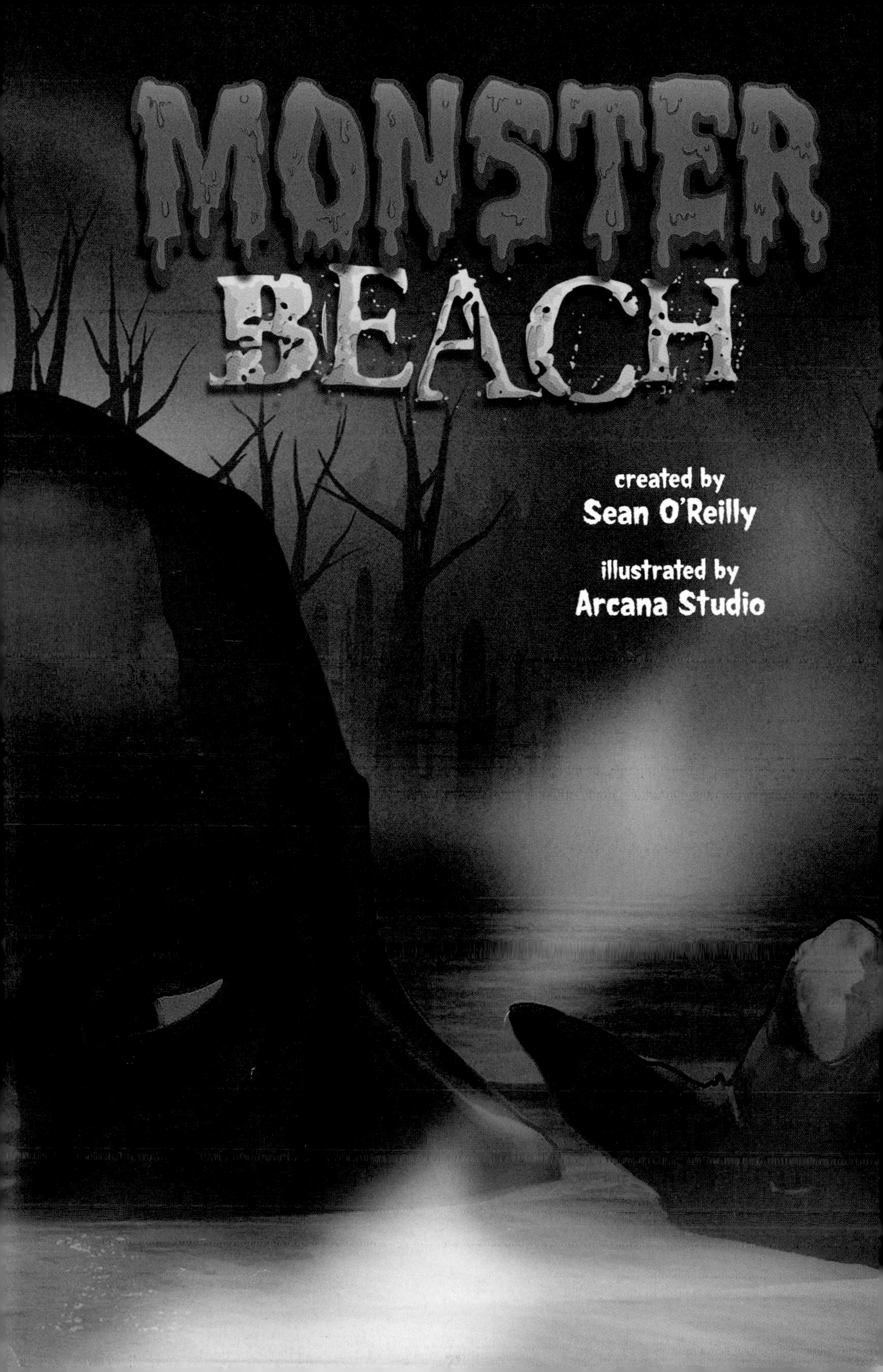

created by
Sean O'Reilly

illustrated by
Arcana Studio

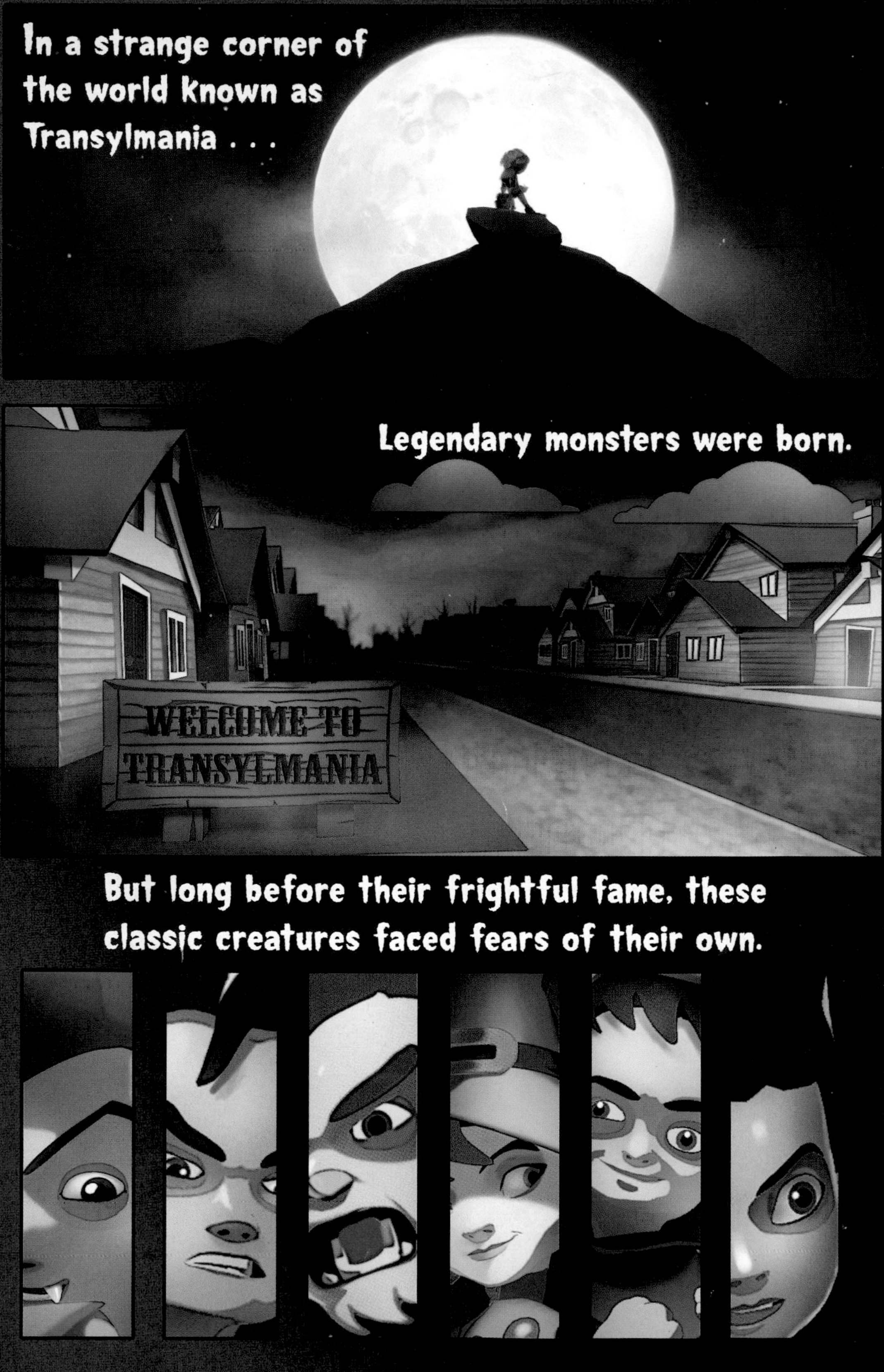
In a strange corner of the world known as Transylmania . . .
Legendary monsters were born.
WELCOME TO TRANSYLMANIA
But long before their frightful fame, these classic creatures faced fears of their own.

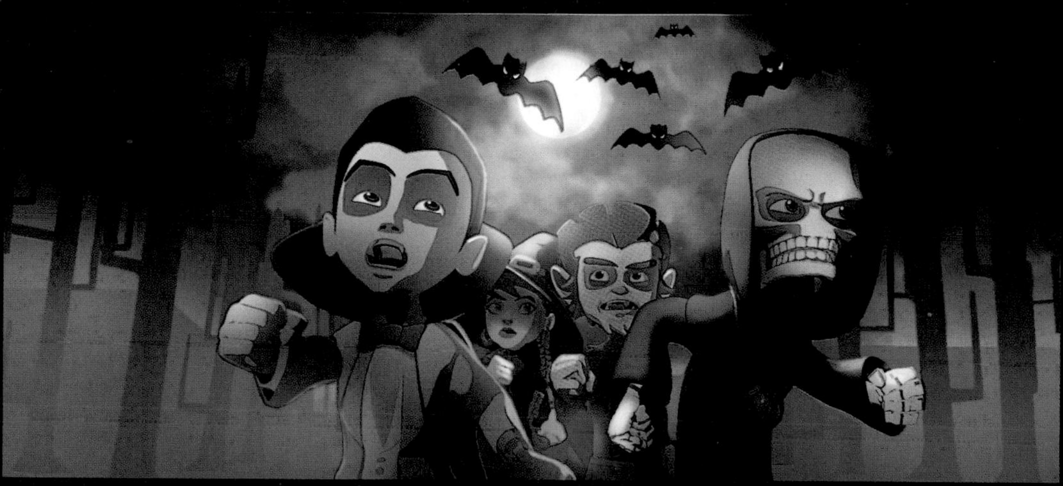

To take on terrifying teachers and homework horrors, they formed the most fearsome friendship on Earth . . .

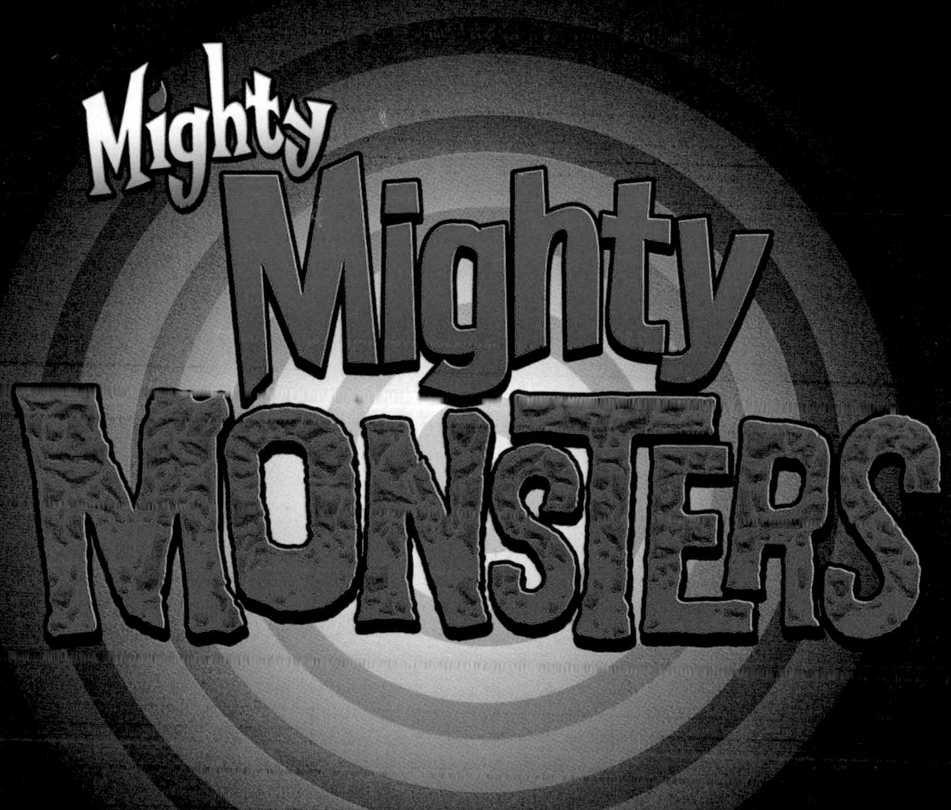
Mighty
Mighty
MONSTERS

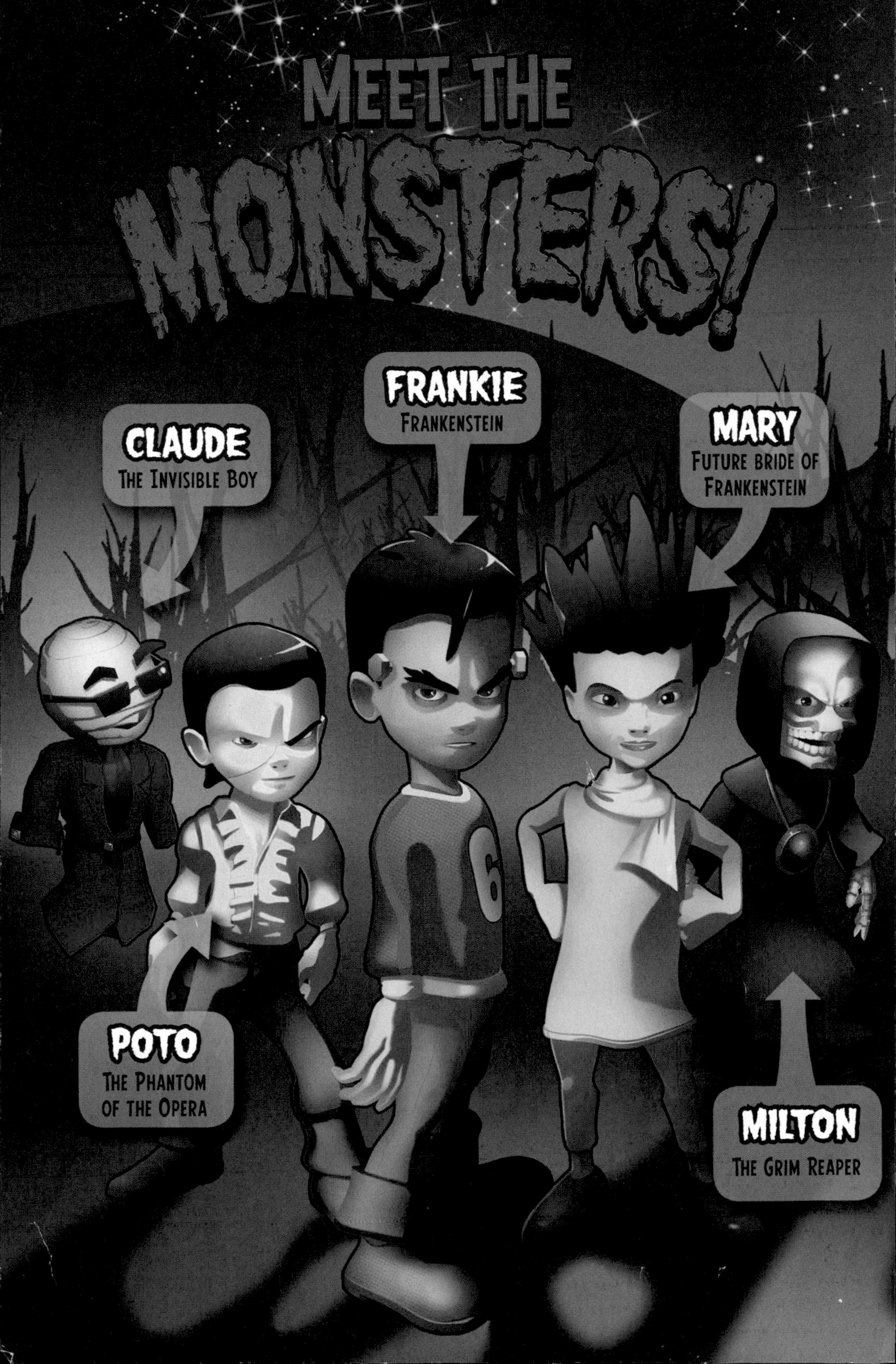
MEET THE MONSTERS!
FRANKIE
FRANKENSTEIN
CLAUDE
THE INVISIBLE BOY
MARY
FUTURE BRIDE OF FRANKENSTEIN
POTO
THE PHANTOM OF THE OPERA
MILTON
THE GRIM REAPER

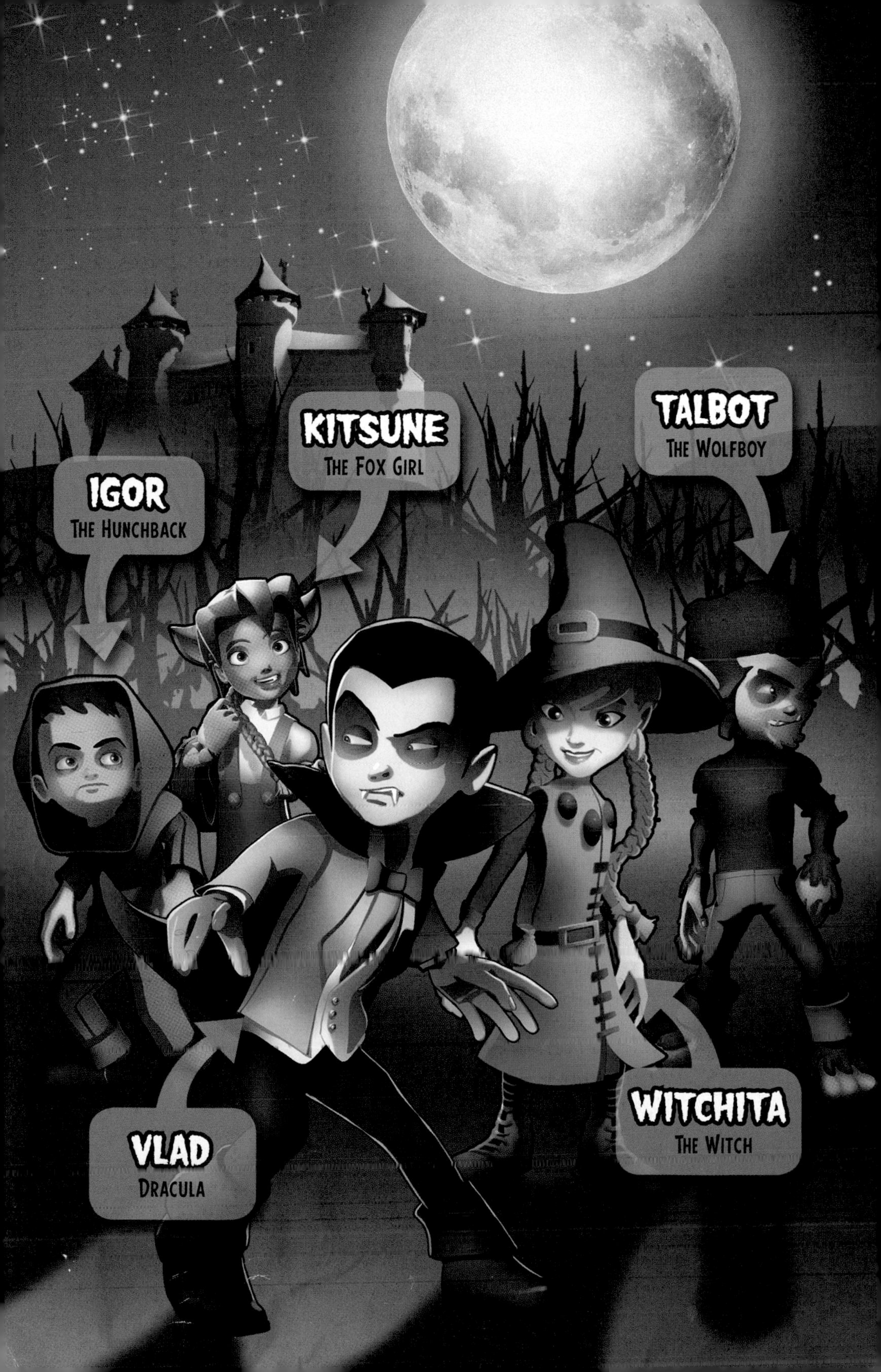

KITSUNE
THE FOX GIRL
TALBOT
THE WOLFBOY
IGOR
THE HUNCHBACK
VLAD
DRACULA
WITCHITA
THE WITCH

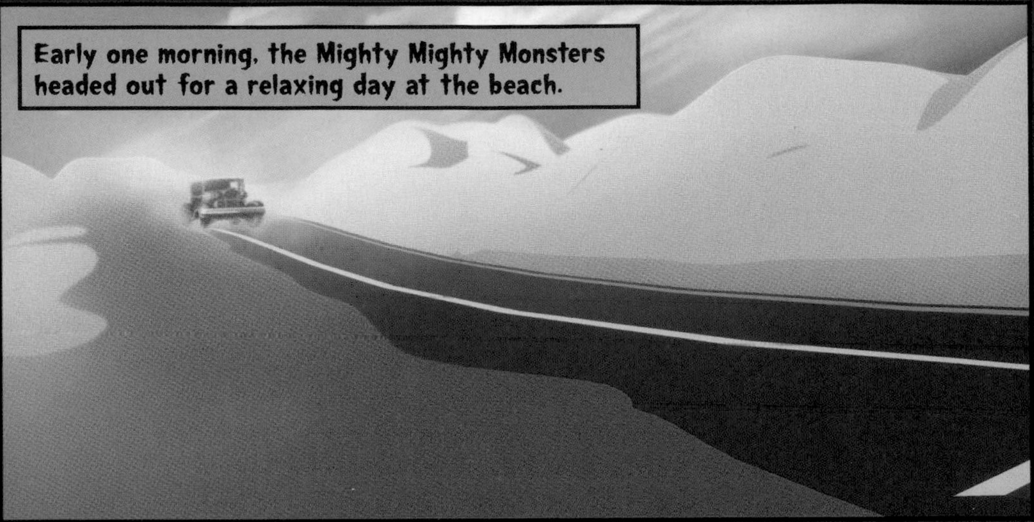
Early one morning, the Mighty Mighty Monsters headed out for a relaxing day at the beach.

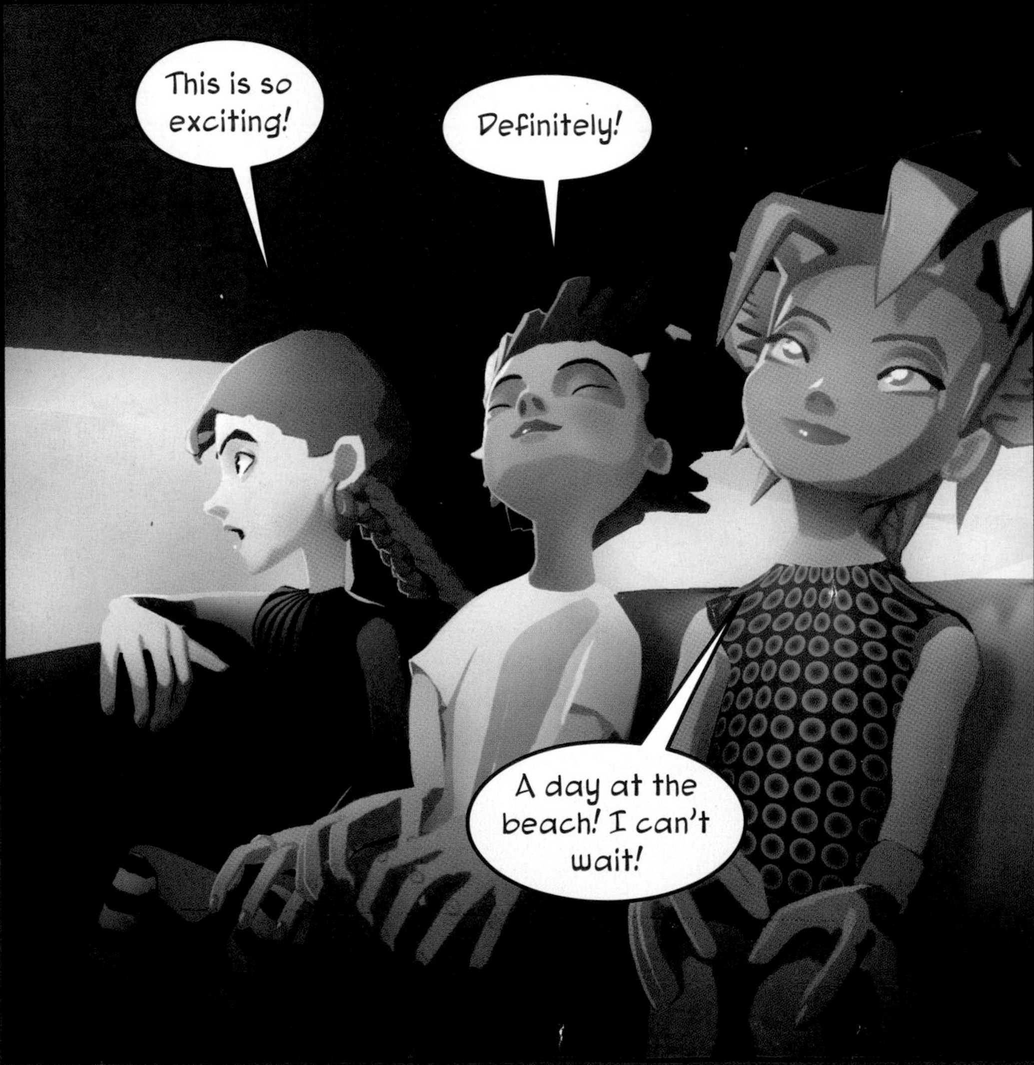
This is so exciting!
Definitely!
A day at the beach! I can't wait!

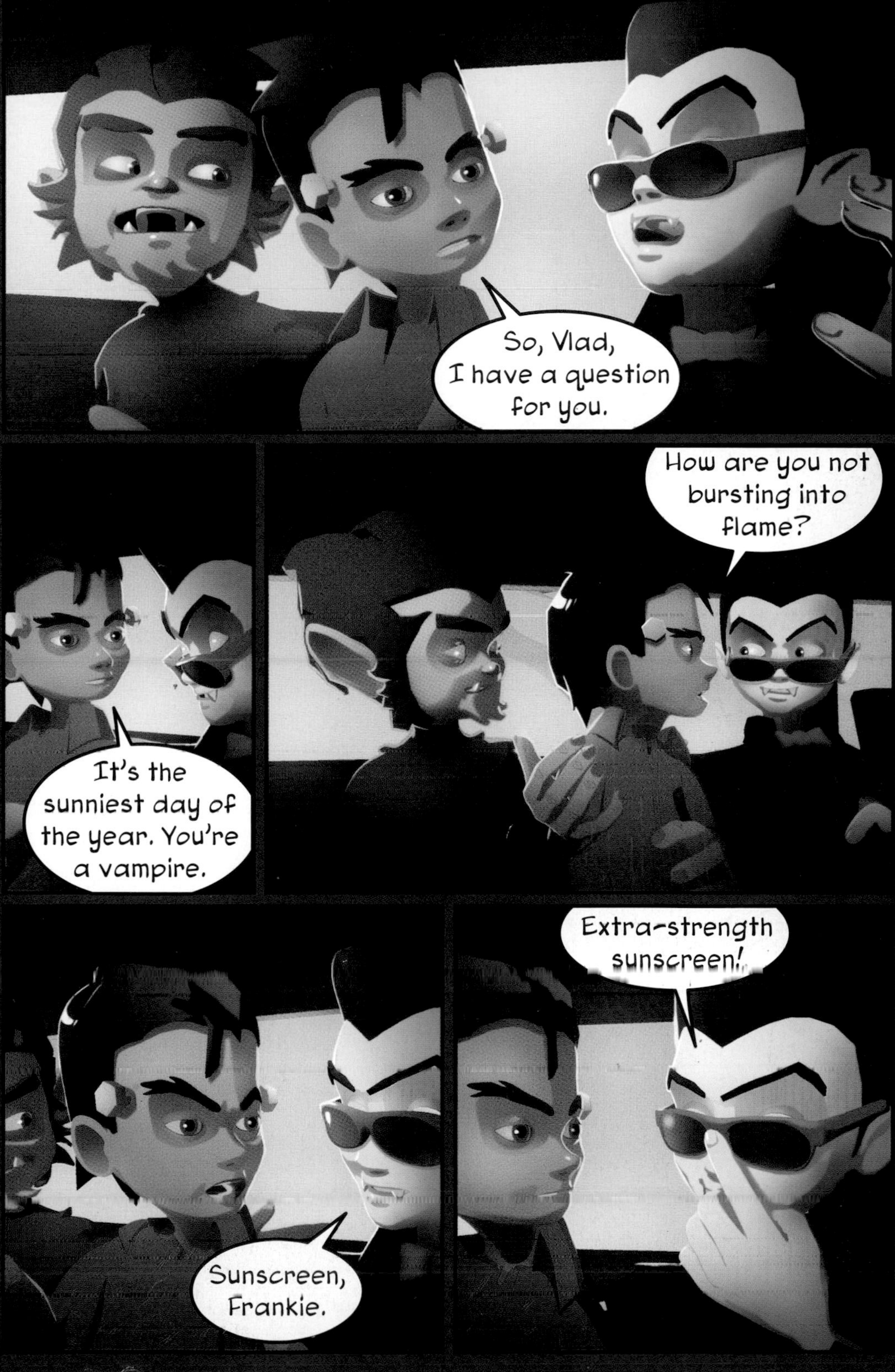
So, Vlad, I have a question for you.
It's the sunniest day of the year. You're a vampire.
How are you not bursting into flame?
Sunscreen, Frankie.
Extra-strength sunscreen!

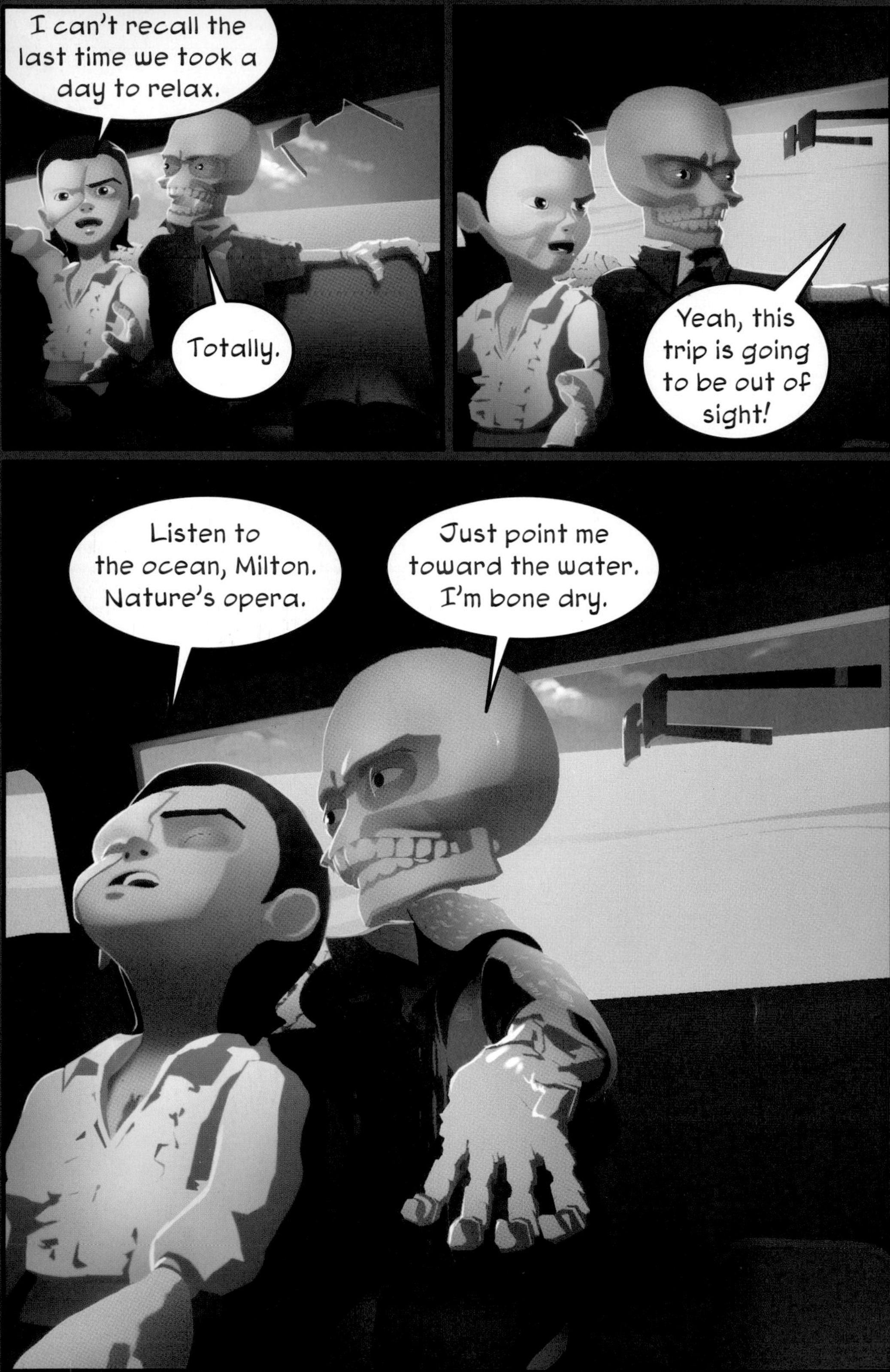
I can't recall the last time we took a day to relax.
Totally.
Yeah, this trip is going to be out of sight!
Listen to the ocean, Milton. Nature's opera.
Just point me toward the water. I'm bone dry.

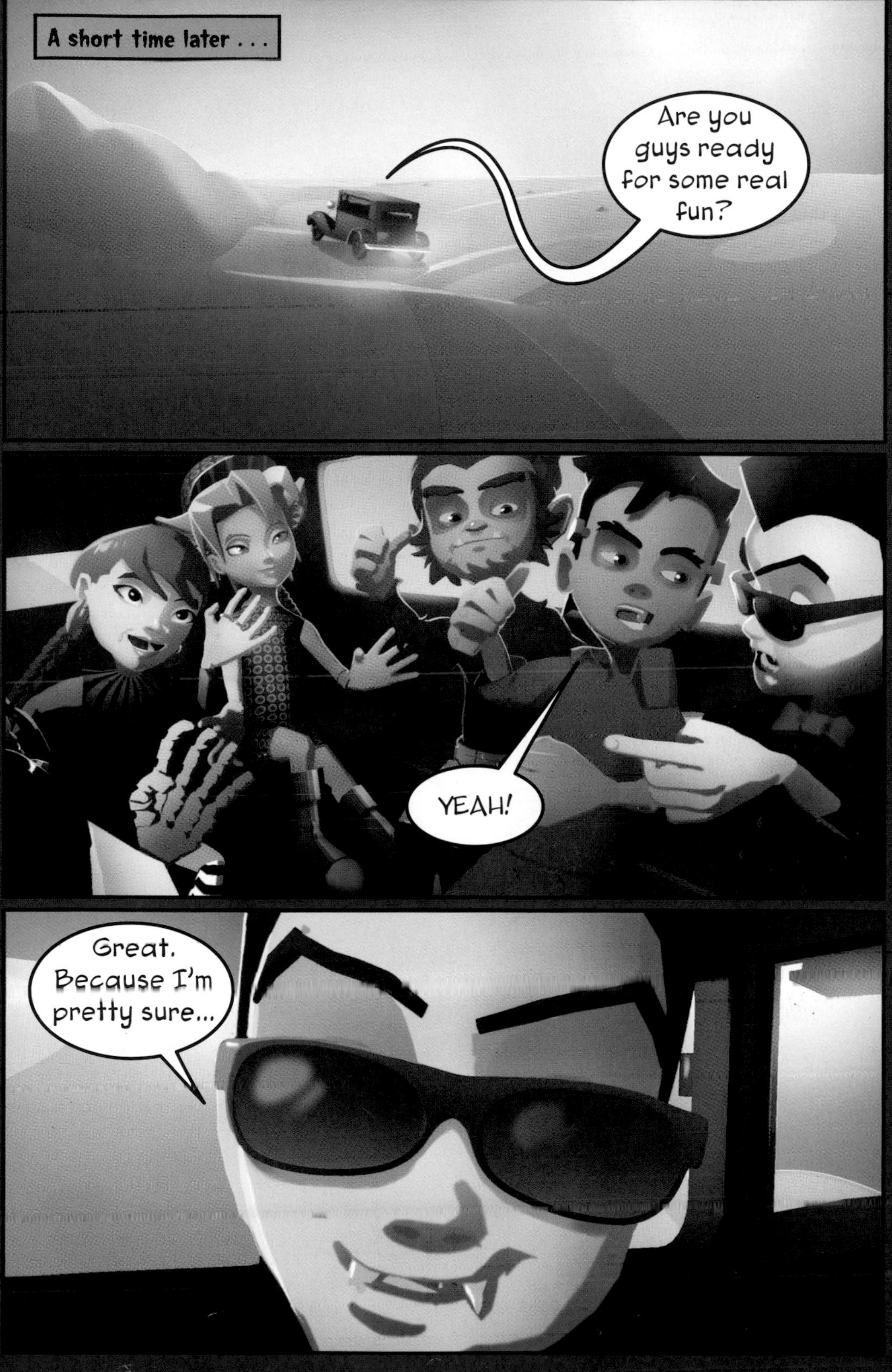

A short time later . . .
Are you guys ready for some real fun?
YEAH!
Great. Because I'm pretty sure...

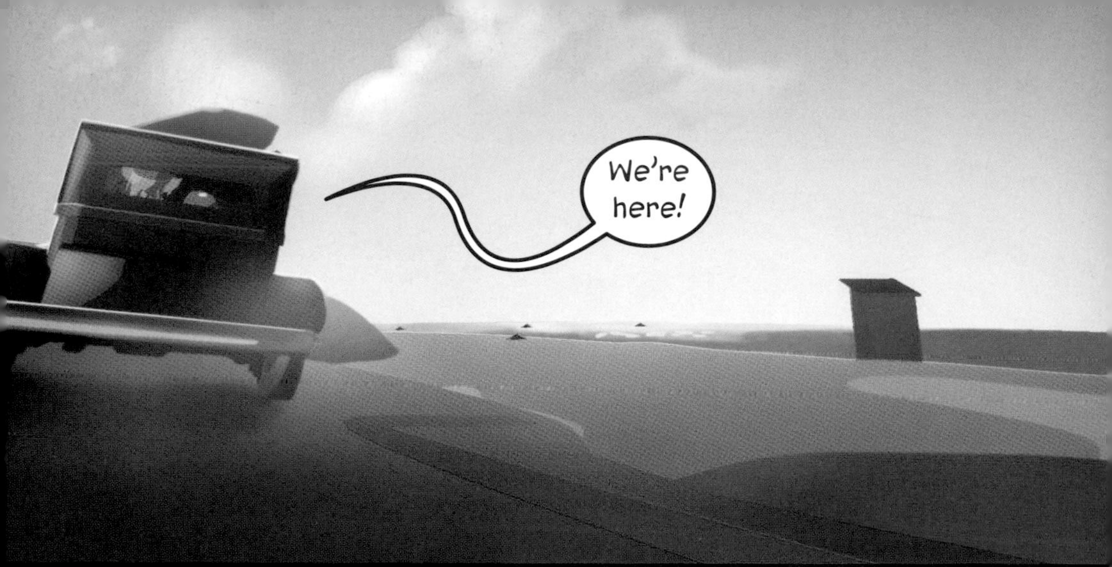
We're here!
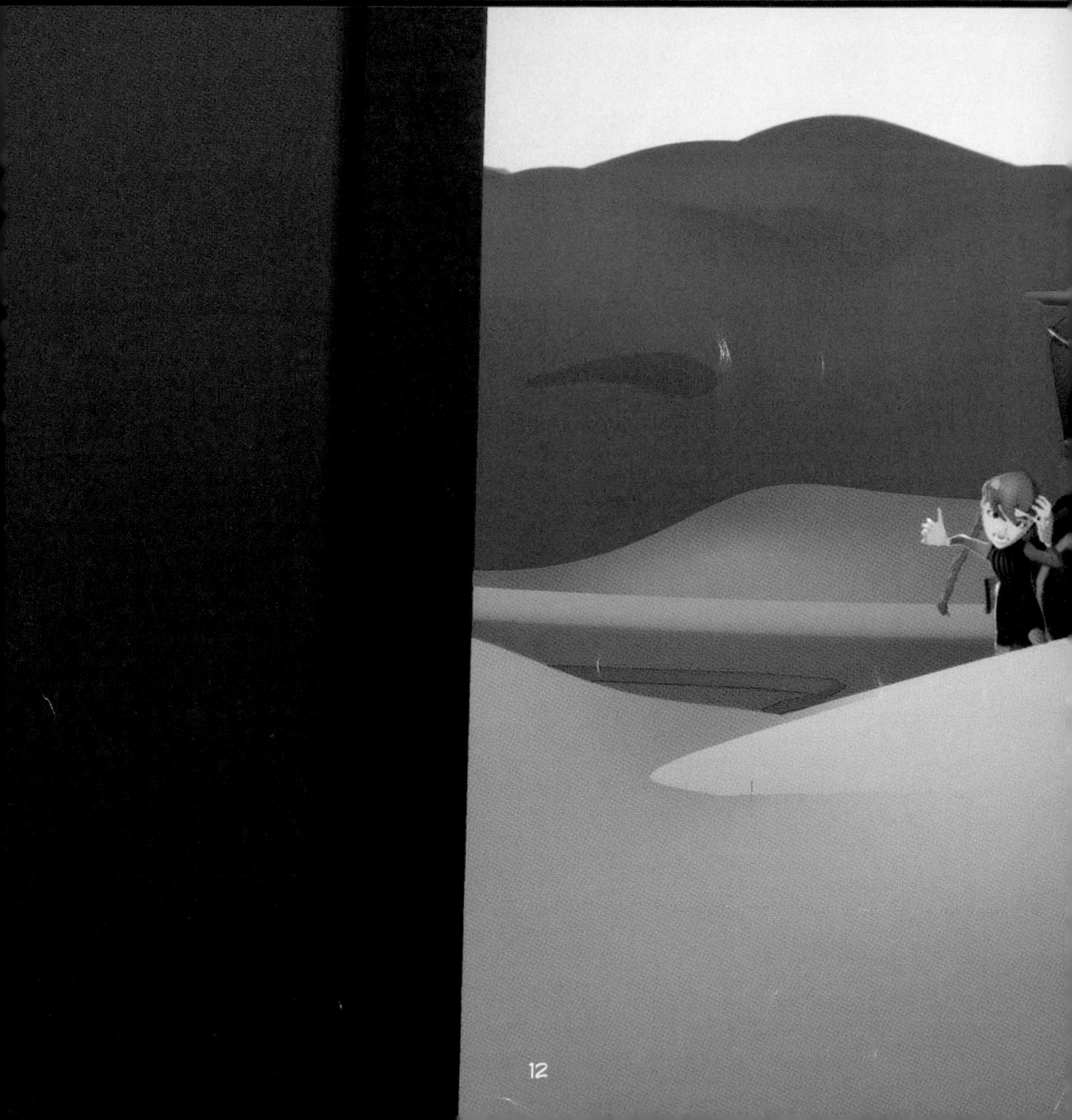

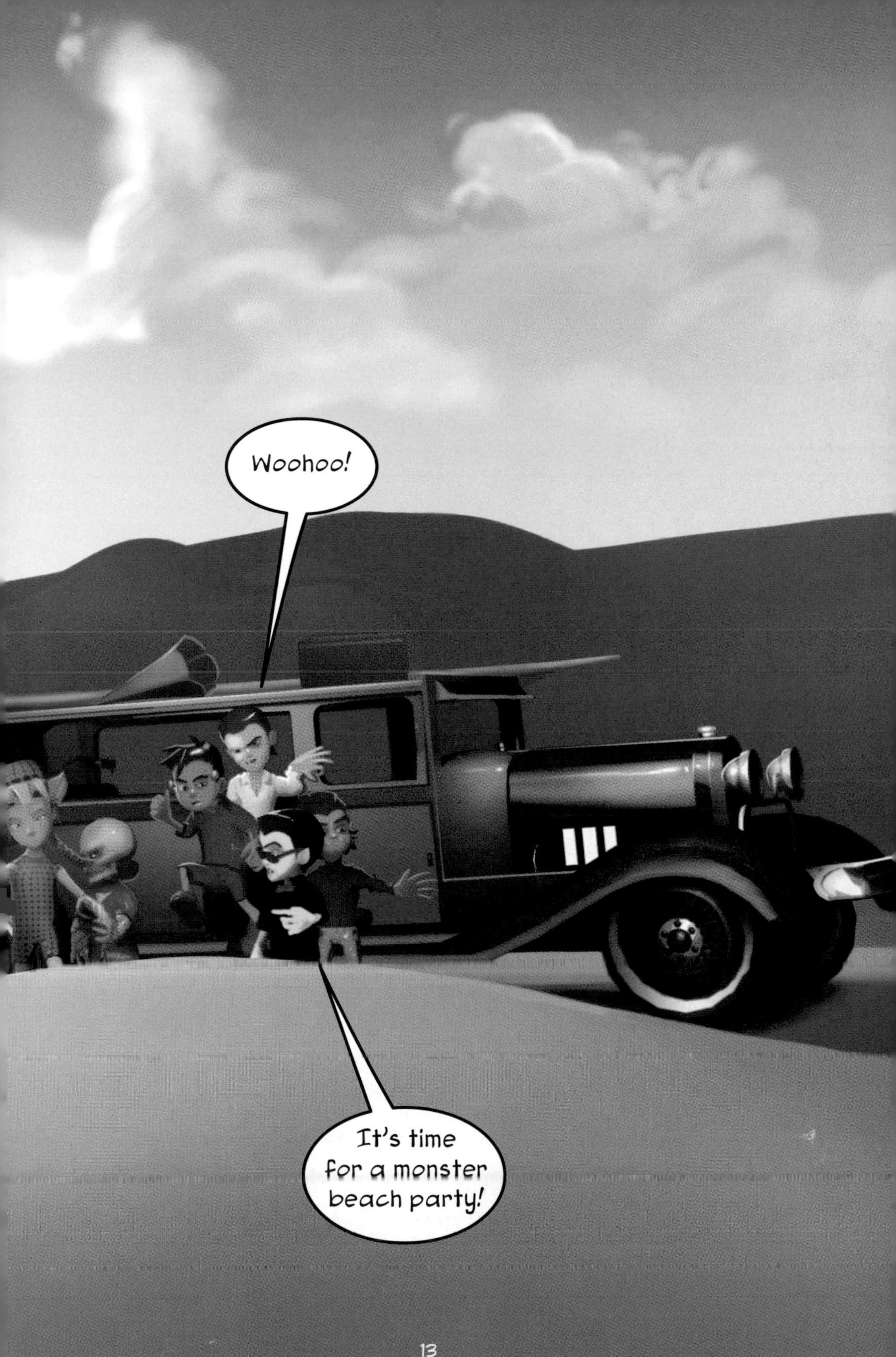
Woohoo!
It's time for a monster beach party!

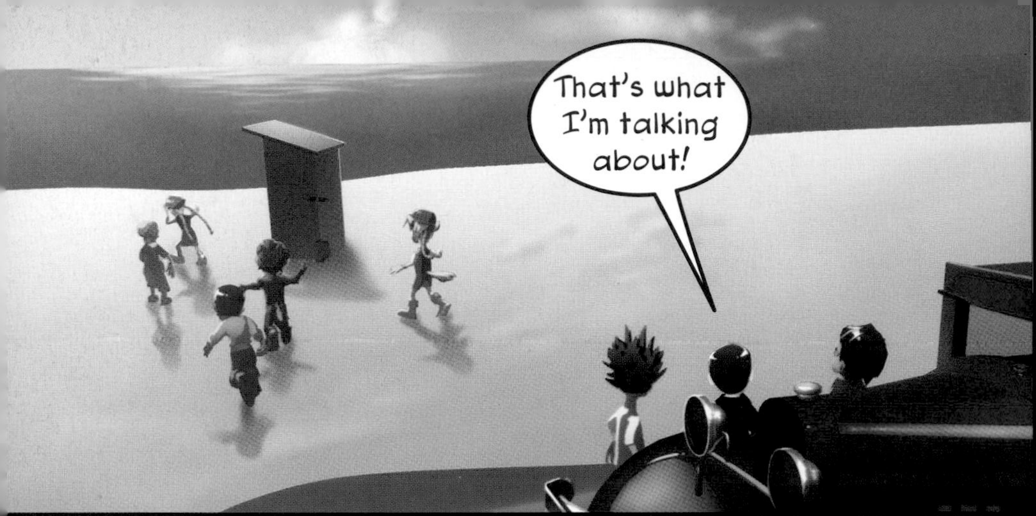
That's what I'm talking about!
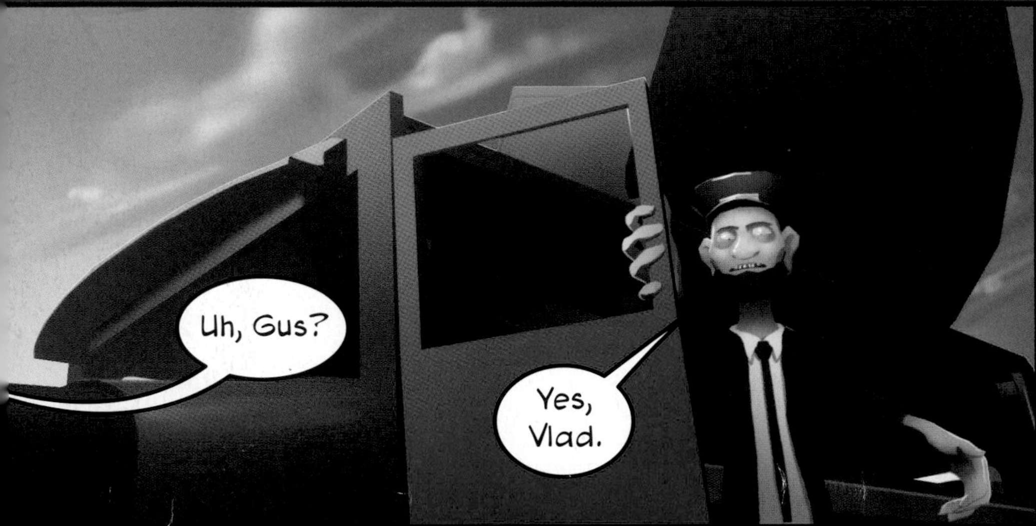
Uh, Gus?
Yes, Vlad.
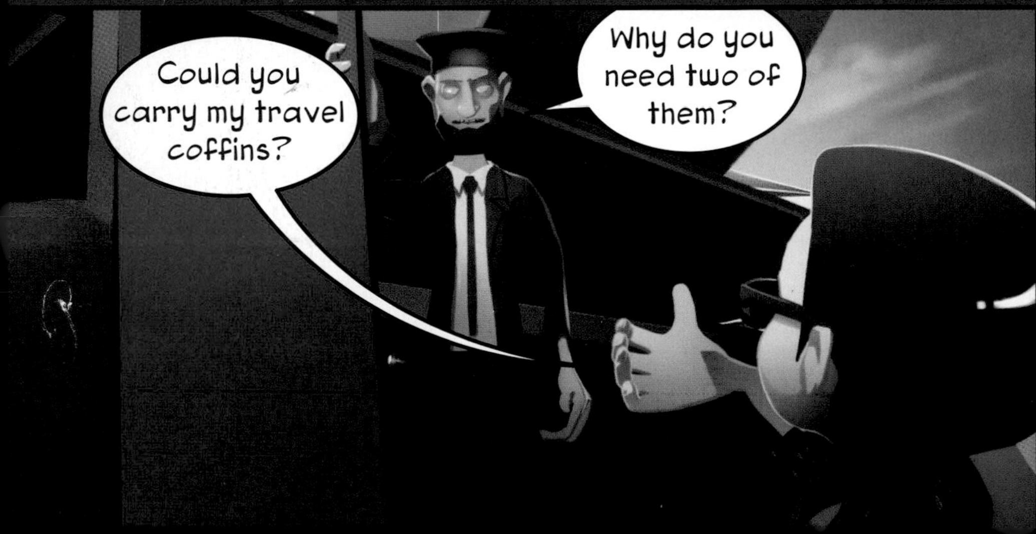
Could you carry my travel coffins?
Why do you need two of them?

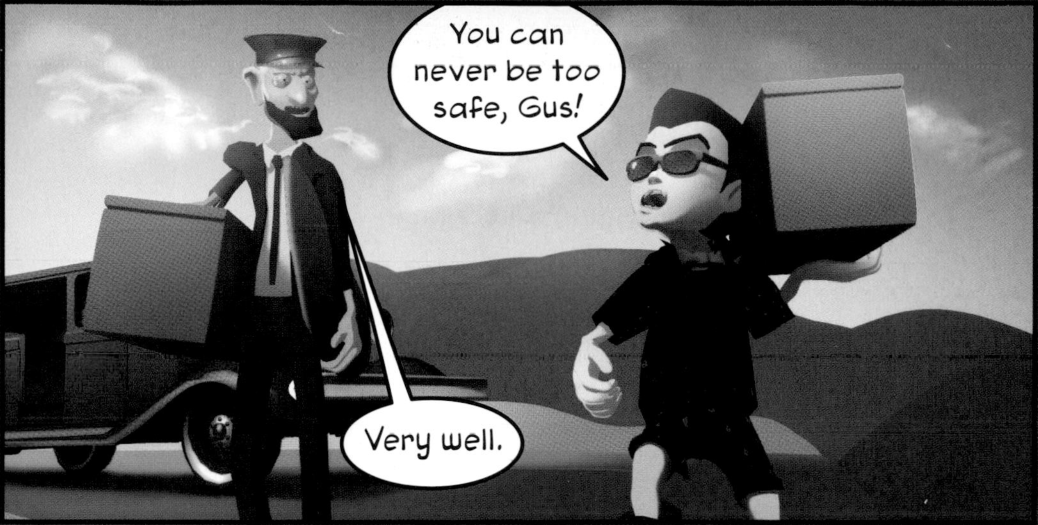
You can never be too safe, Gus!
Very well.

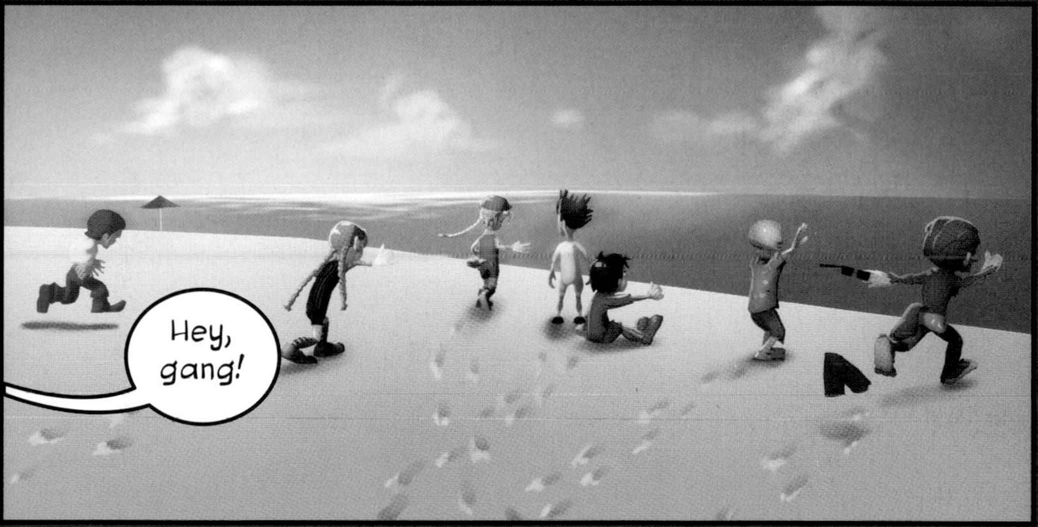
Hey, gang!

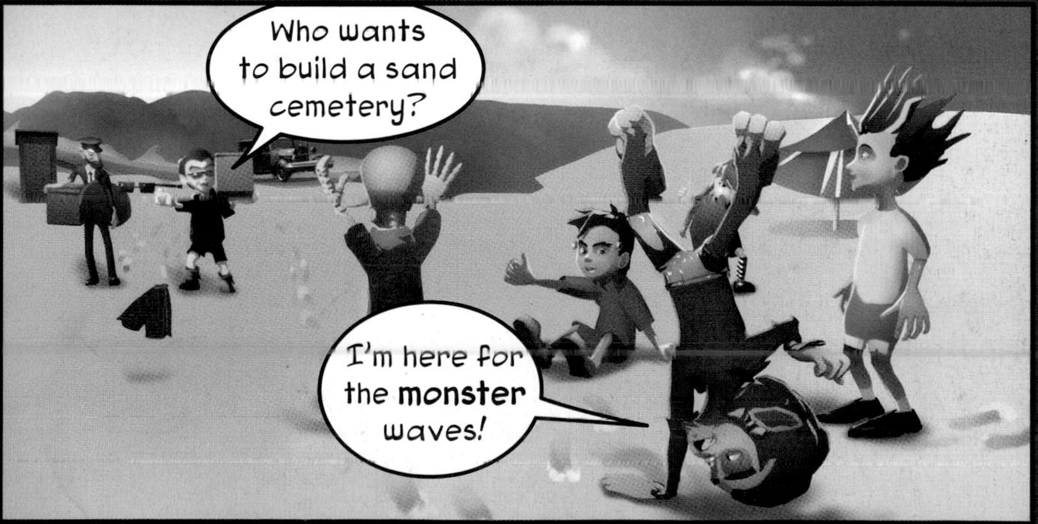
Who wants to build a sand cemetery?
I'm here for the **monster** waves!

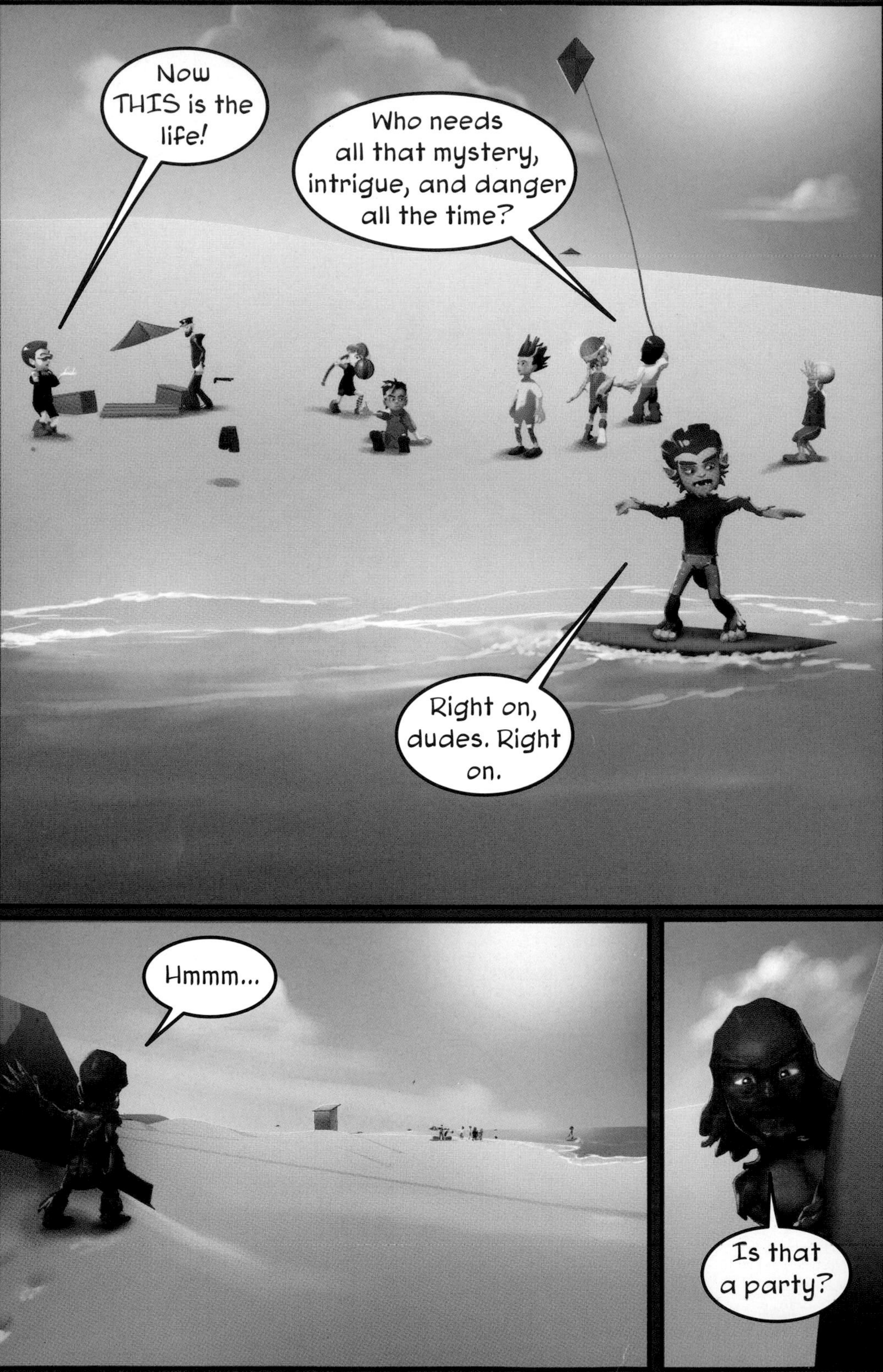
Now THIS is the life!
Who needs all that mystery, intrigue, and danger all the time?
Right on, dudes. Right on.
Hmmm...
Is that a party?

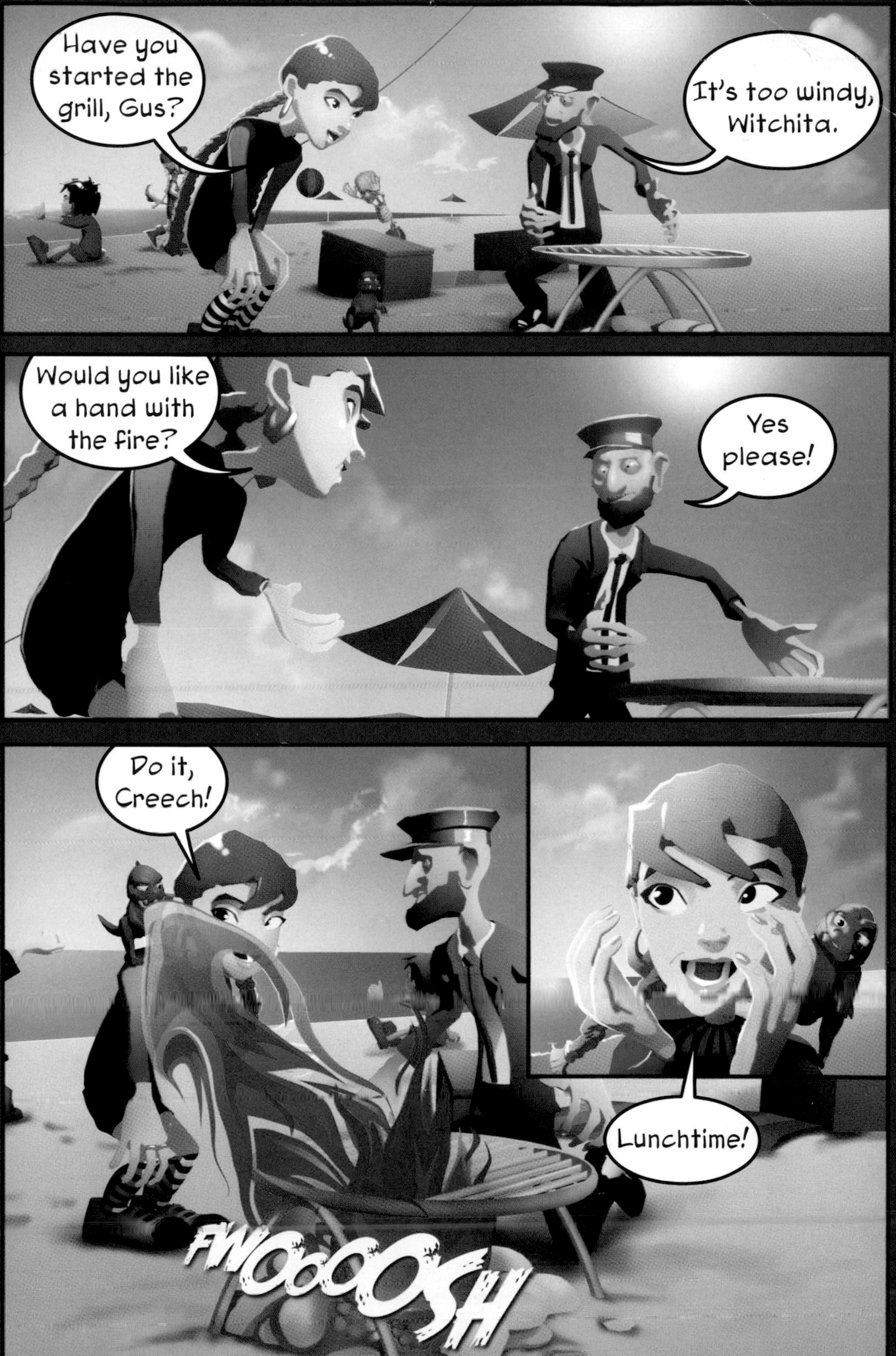
Have you started the grill, Gus?
It's too windy, Witchita.
Would you like a hand with the fire?
Yes please!
Do it, Creech!
FWOOOOSH
Lunchtime!

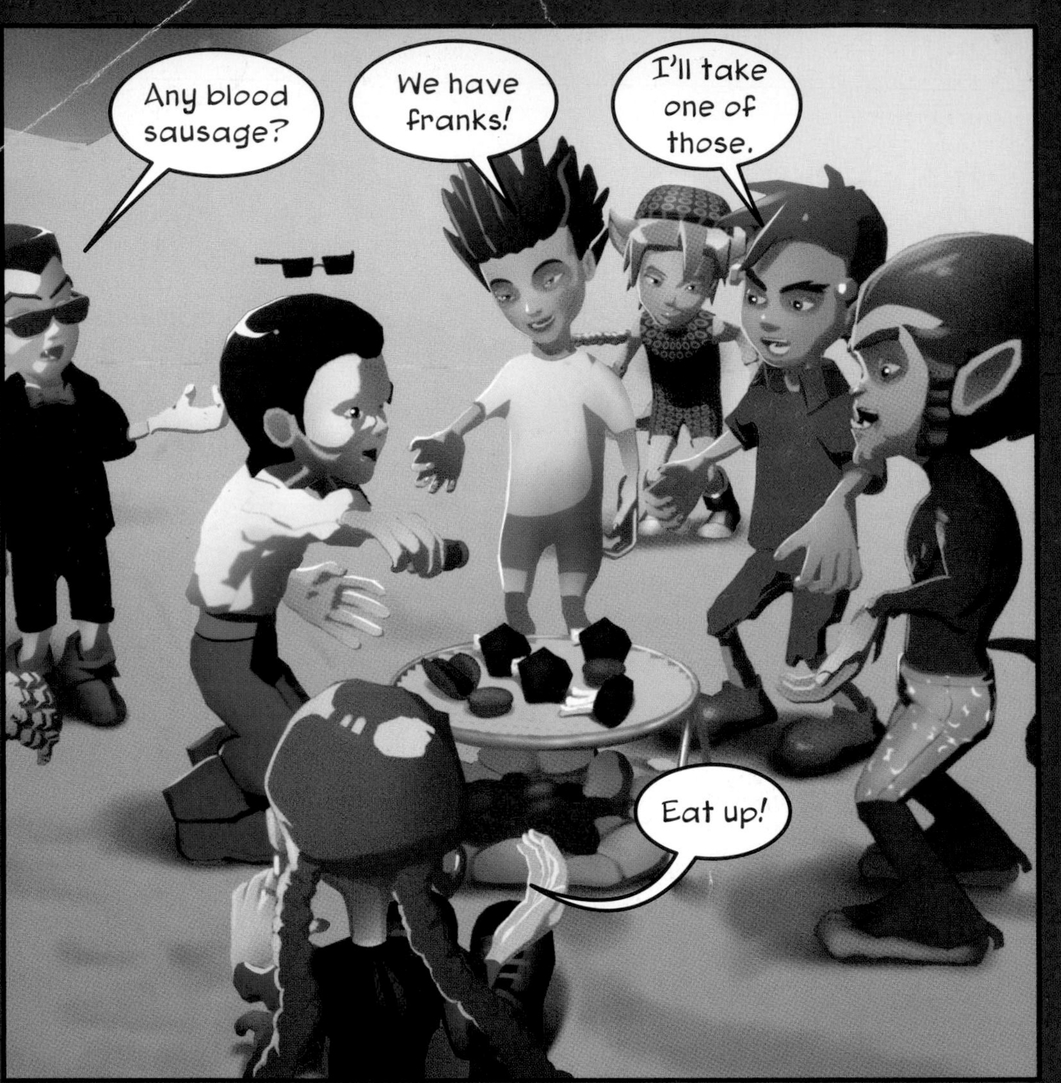
Any blood sausage?
We have franks!
I'll take one of those.
Eat up!

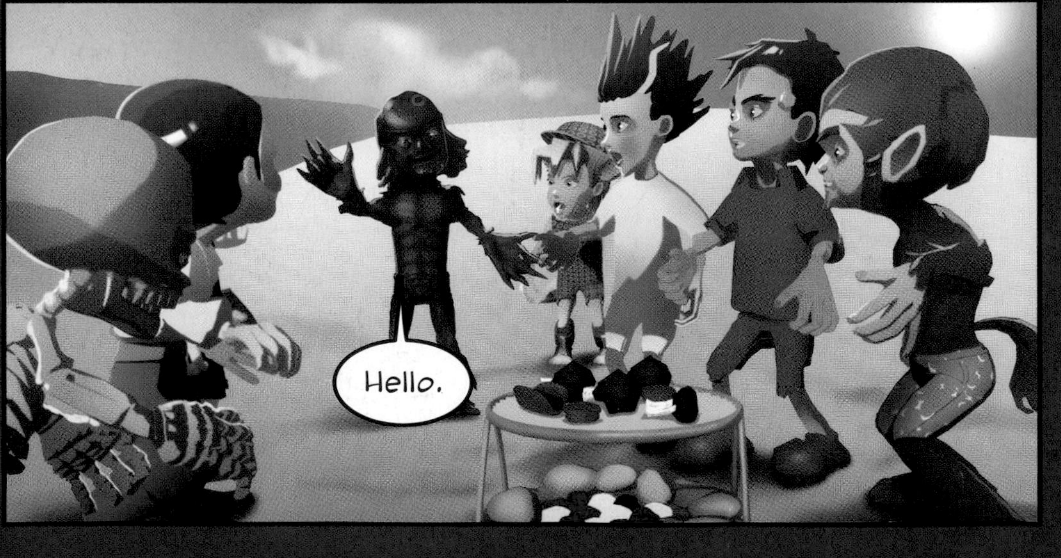
Hello.

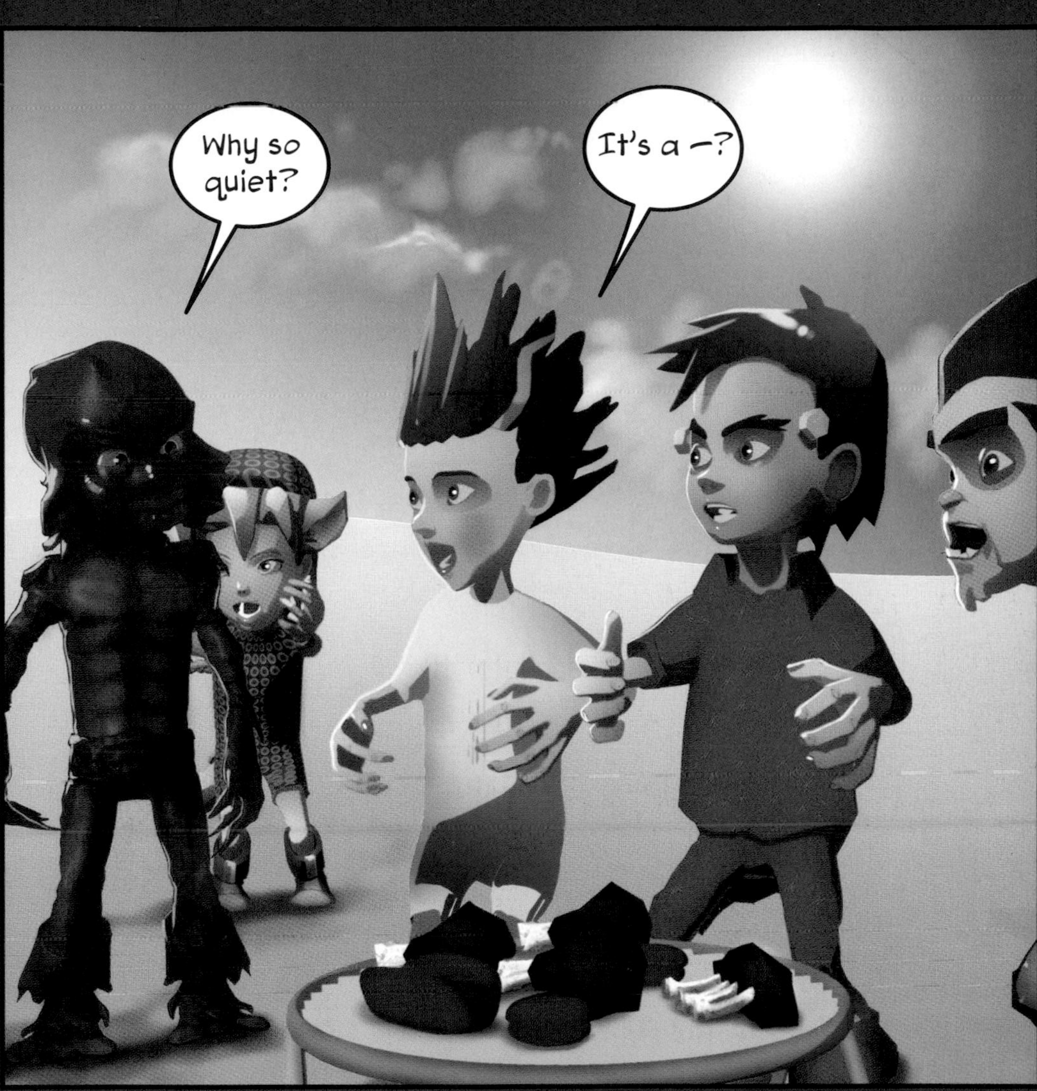
Why so quiet?
It's a –?

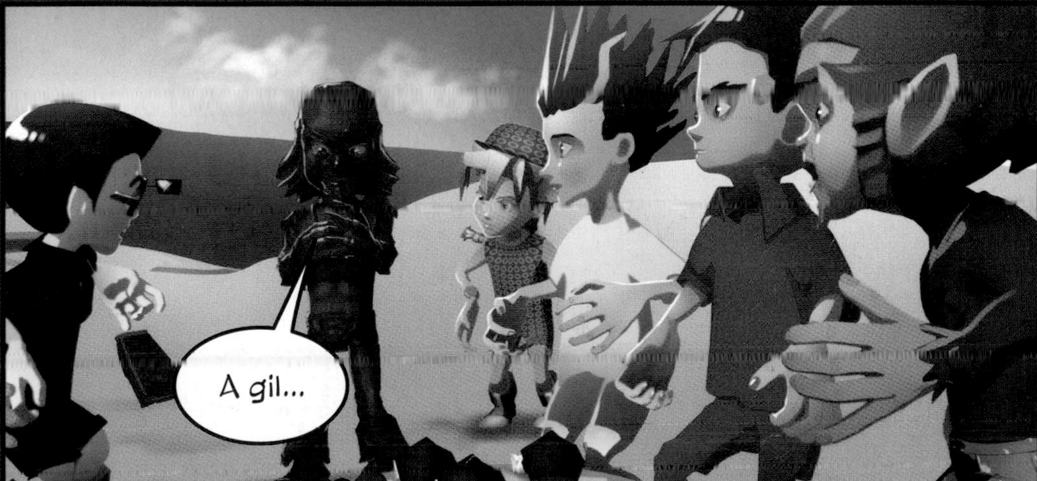
A gil...

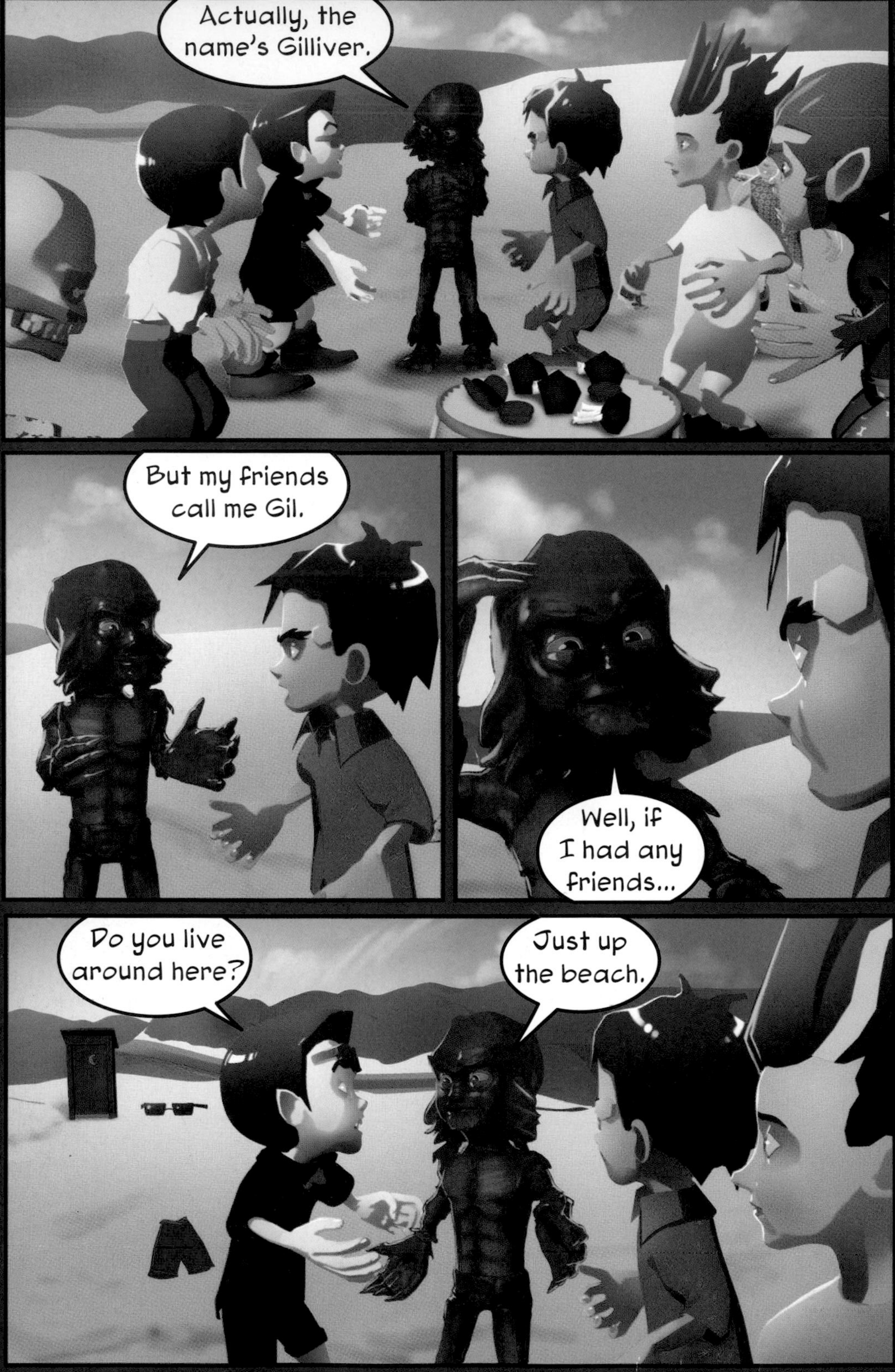
Actually, the name's Gilliver.
But my friends call me Gil.
Well, if I had any friends...
Do you live around here?
Just up the beach.

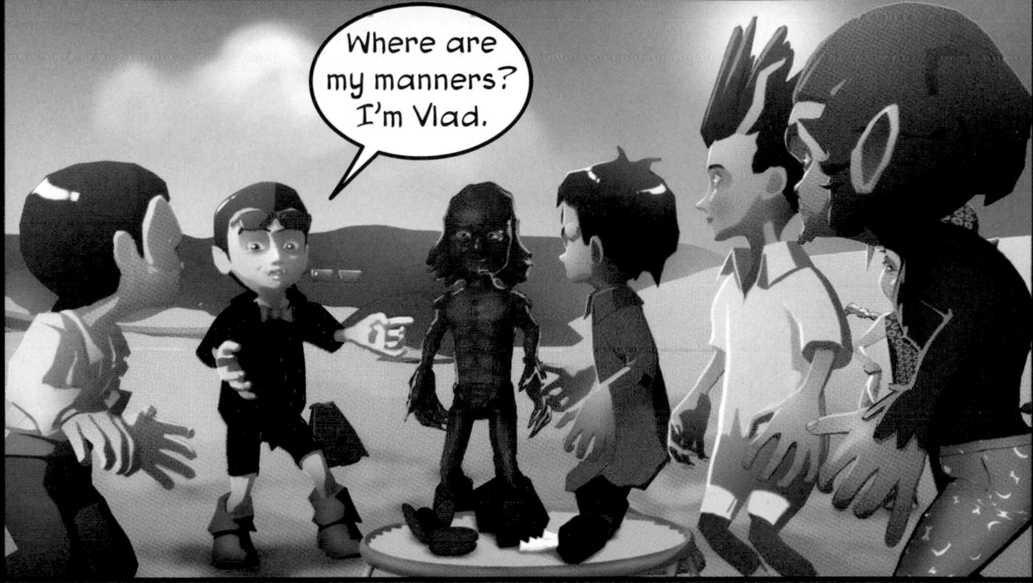
Where are my manners? I'm Vlad.

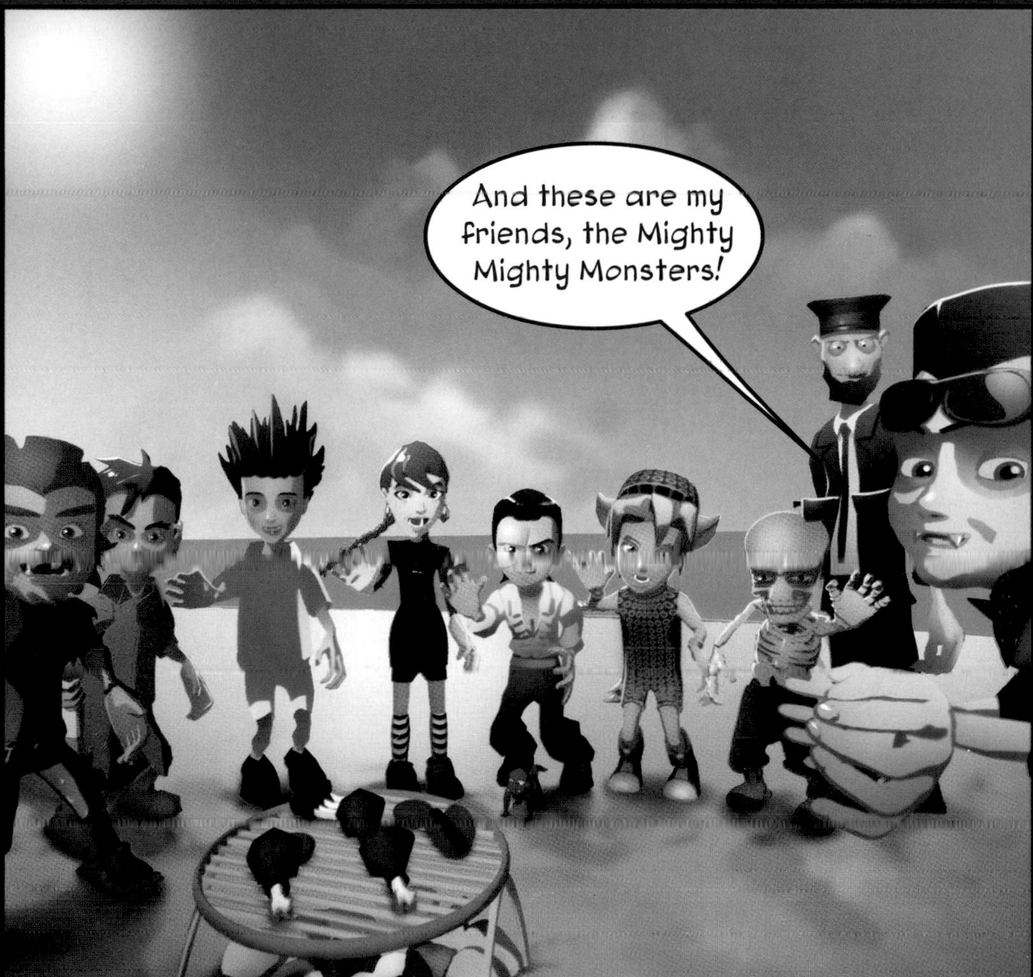
And these are my friends, the Mighty Mighty Monsters!

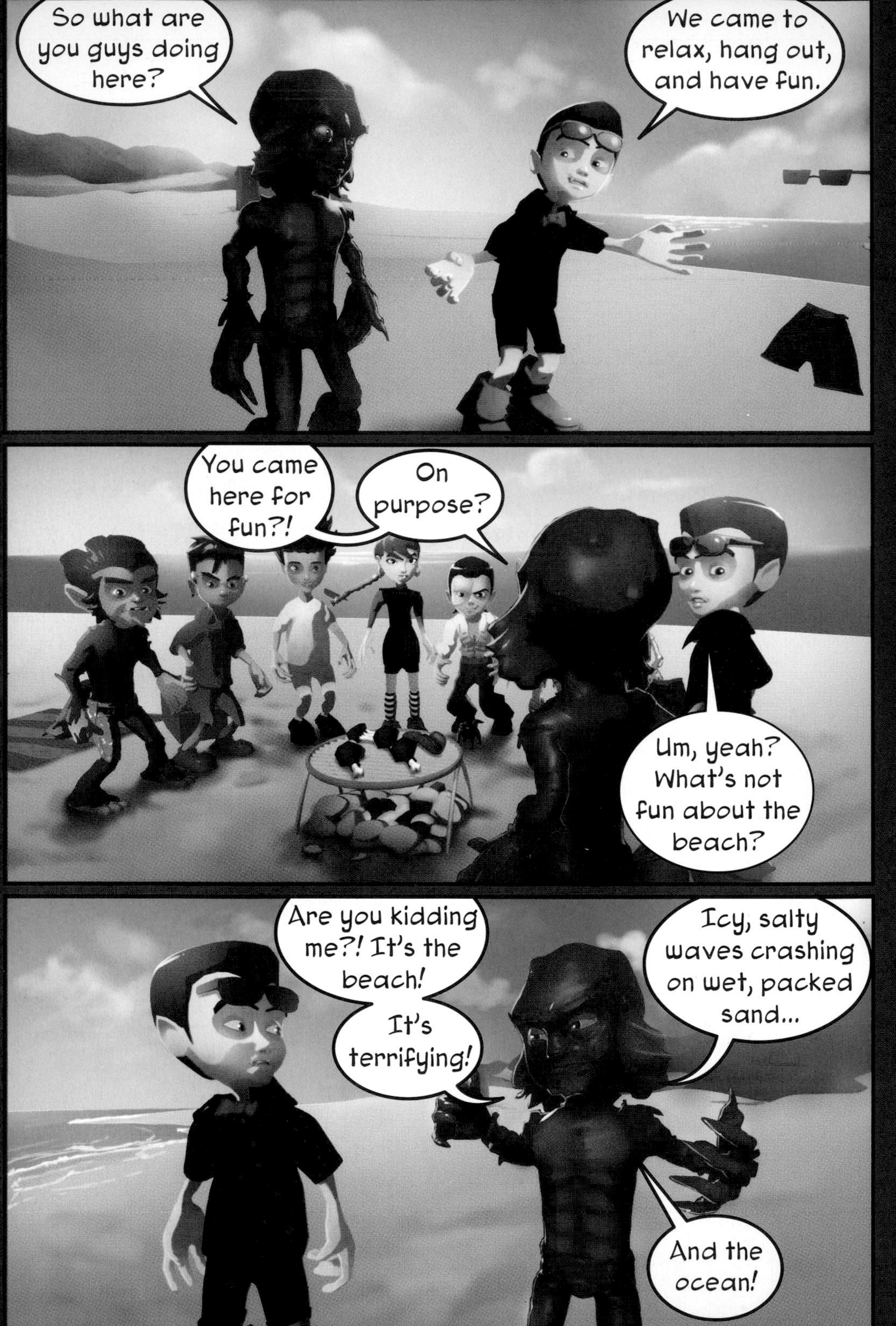
So what are you guys doing here?
We came to relax, hang out, and have fun.
You came here for fun?!
On purpose?
Um, yeah? What's not fun about the beach?
Are you kidding me?! It's the beach!
It's terrifying!
Icy, salty waves crashing on wet, packed sand...
And the ocean!

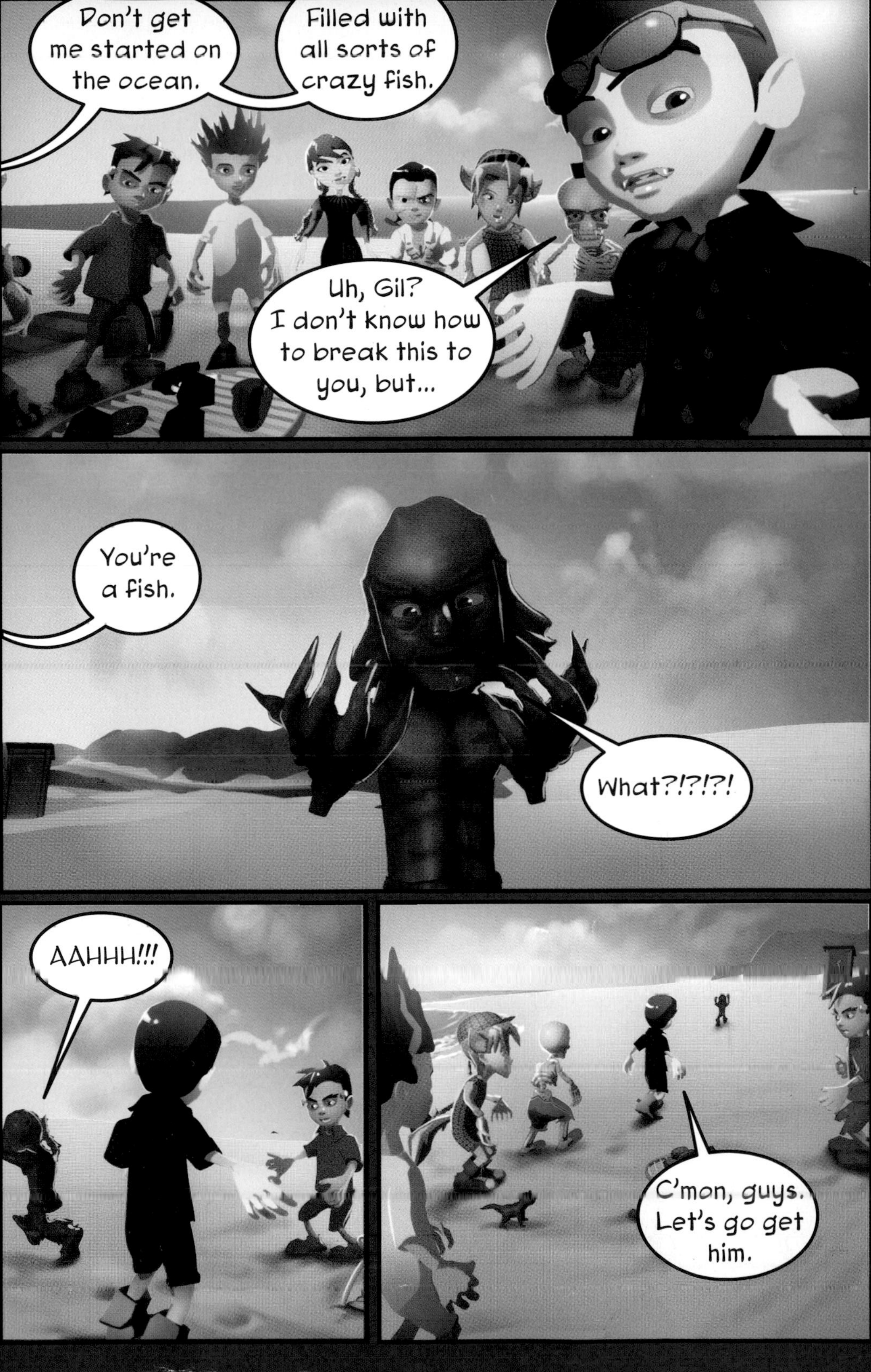
Don't get me started on the ocean.
Filled with all sorts of crazy fish.
Uh, Gil? I don't know how to break this to you, but...
You're a fish.
What?!?!?!
AAHHH!!!
C'mon, guys. Let's go get him.

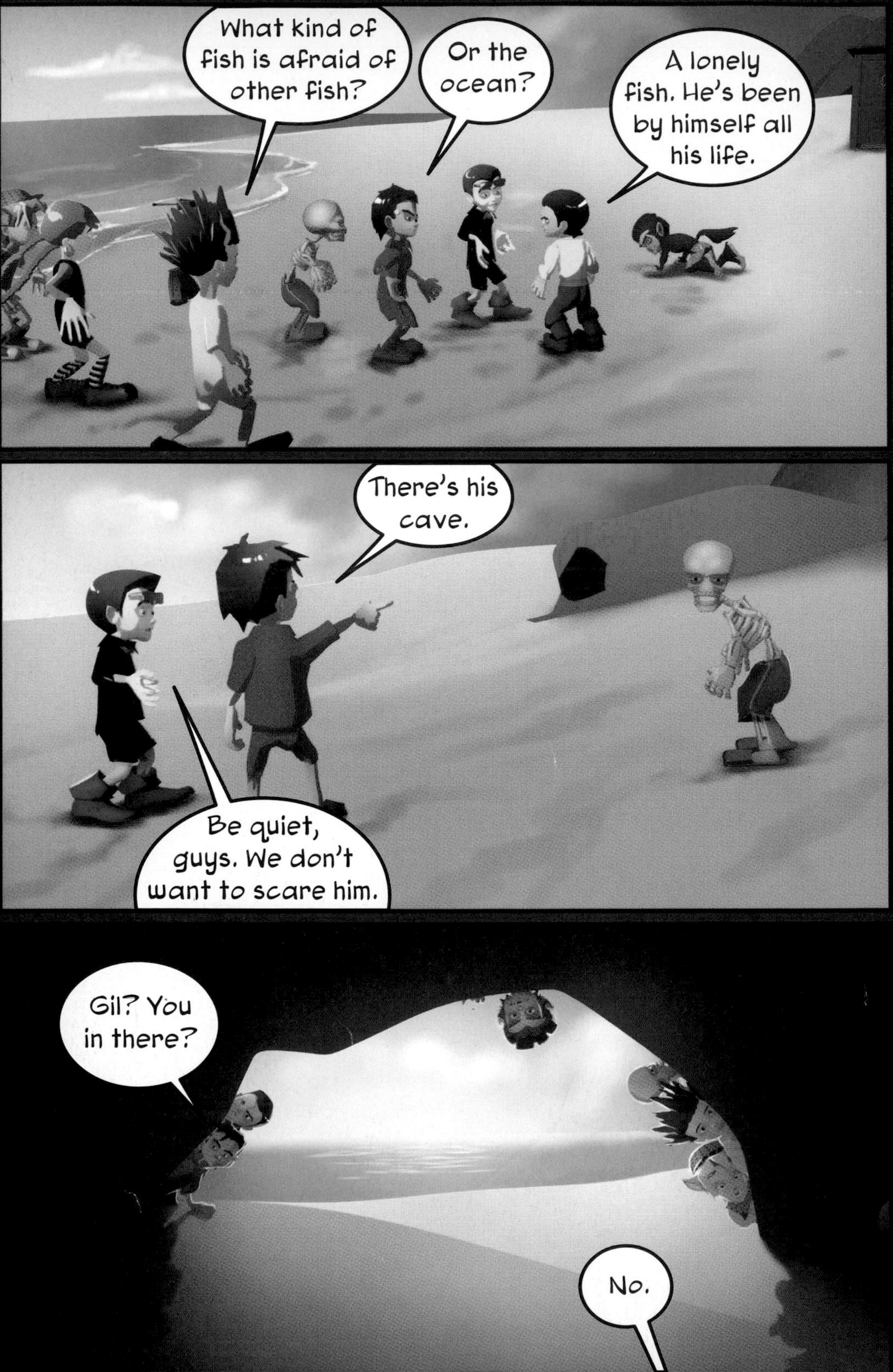
What kind of fish is afraid of other fish?
Or the ocean?
A lonely fish. He's been by himself all his life.
There's his cave.
Be quiet, guys. We don't want to scare him.
Gil? You in there?
No.

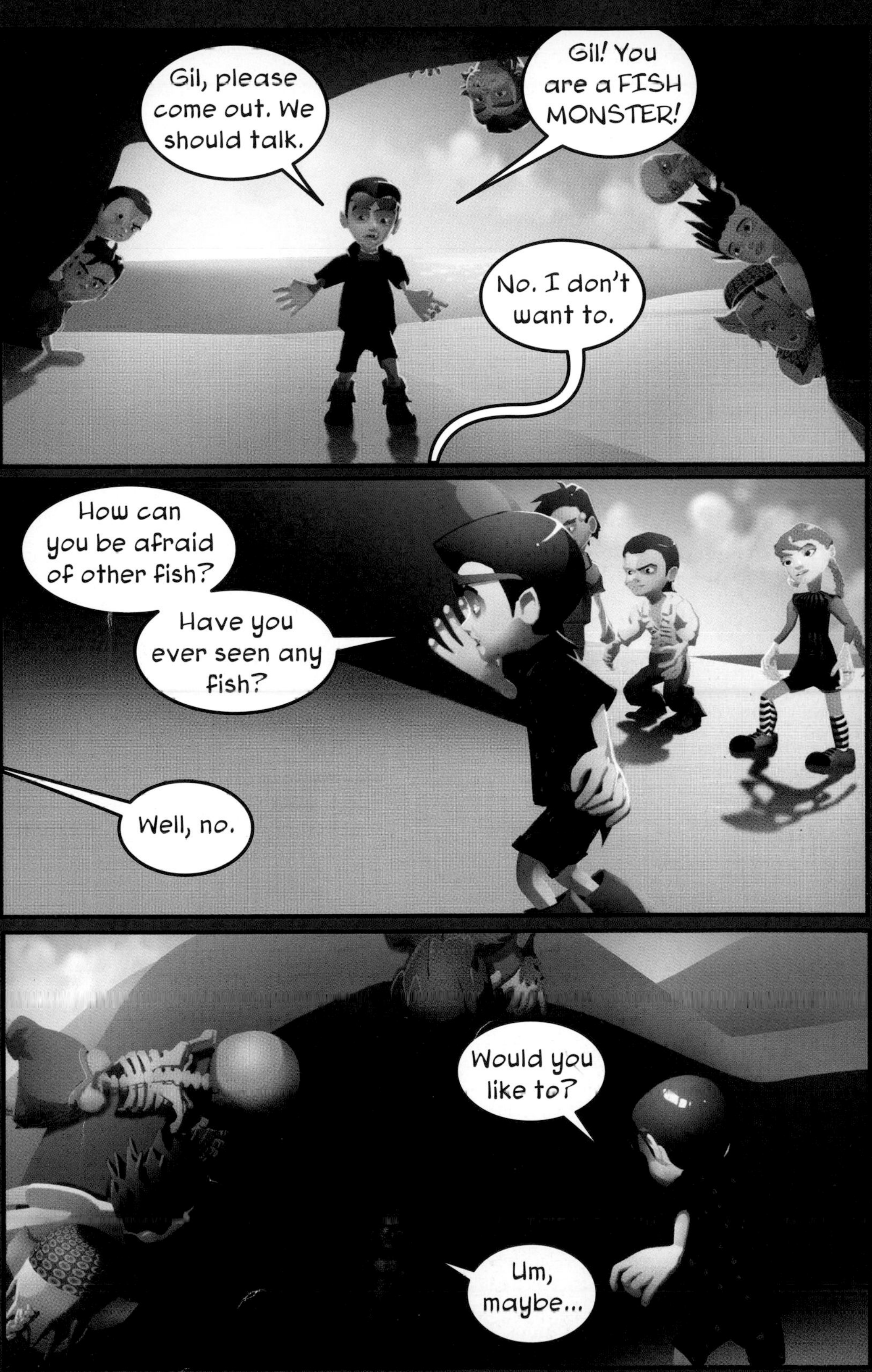
Gil, please come out. We should talk.
Gil! You are a FISH MONSTER!
No. I don't want to.
How can you be afraid of other fish?
Have you ever seen any fish?
Well, no.
Would you like to?
Um, maybe...

Well then. Let's do this!

Witchita, a little magic please.

No problem, my friend.

The sea awaits with fish and fun. But we are made for land and sun.

If our breath we wish to keep, Make equipment for the deep!

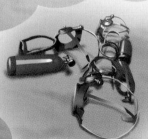

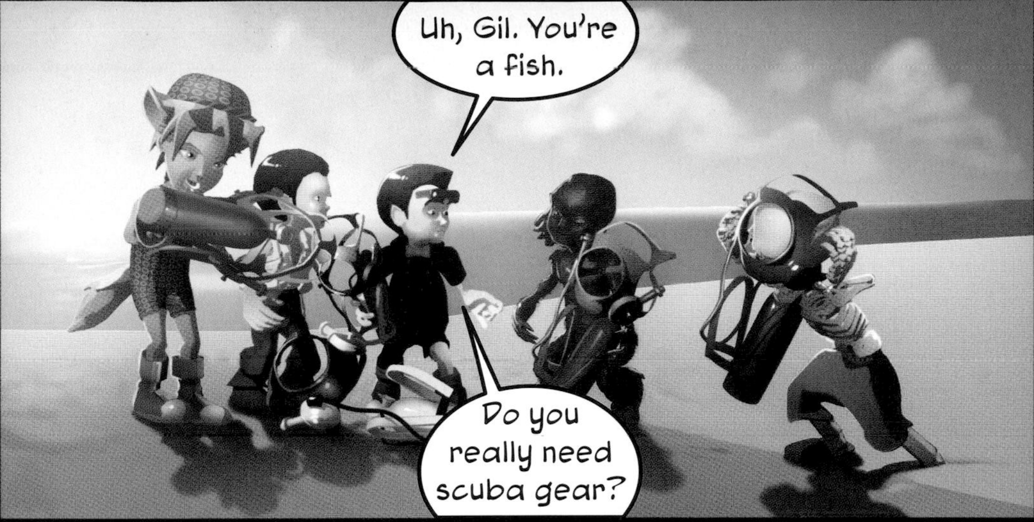
Uh, Gil. You're a fish.
Do you really need scuba gear?

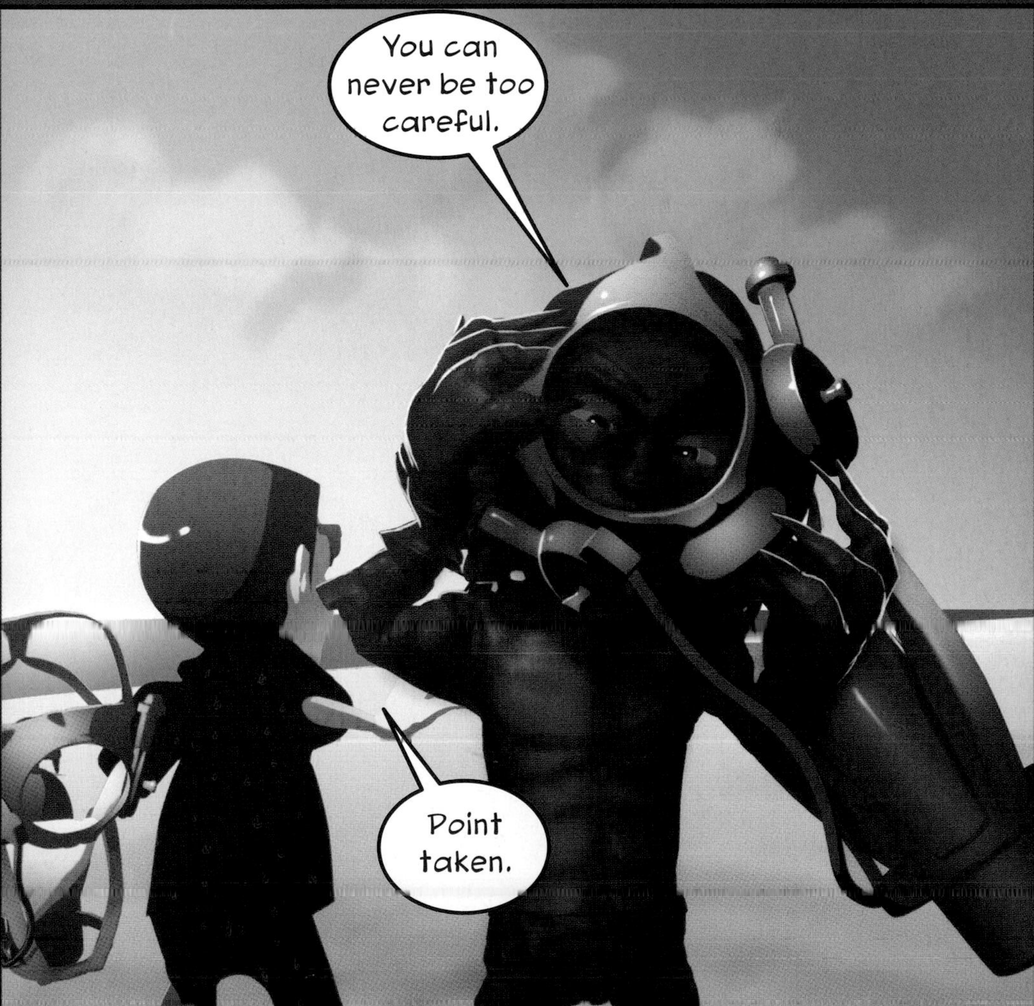
You can never be too careful.
Point taken.

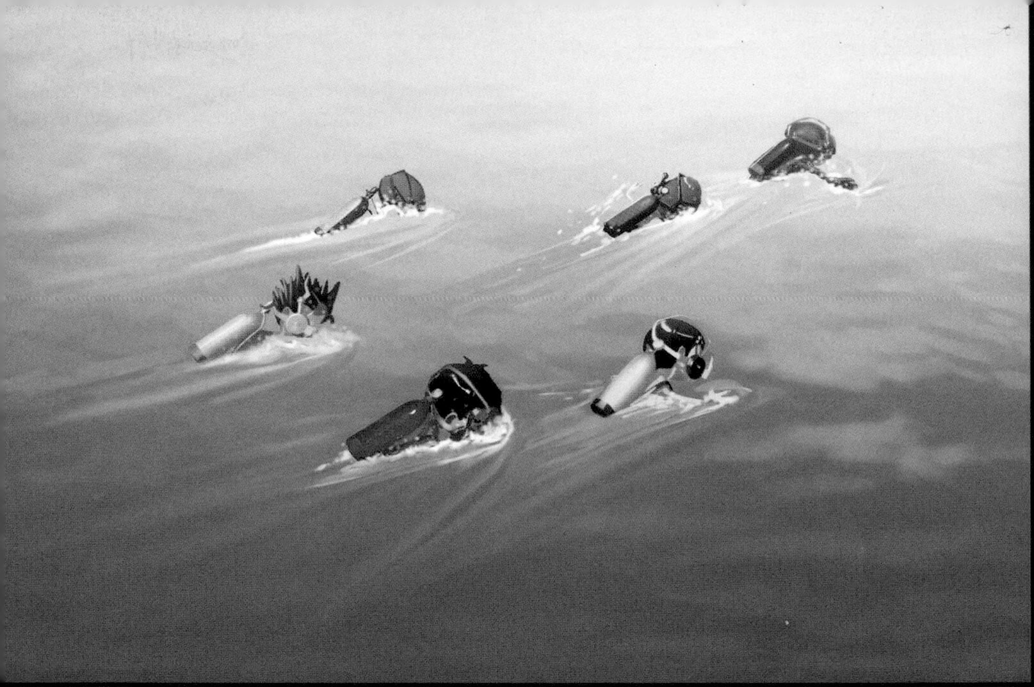

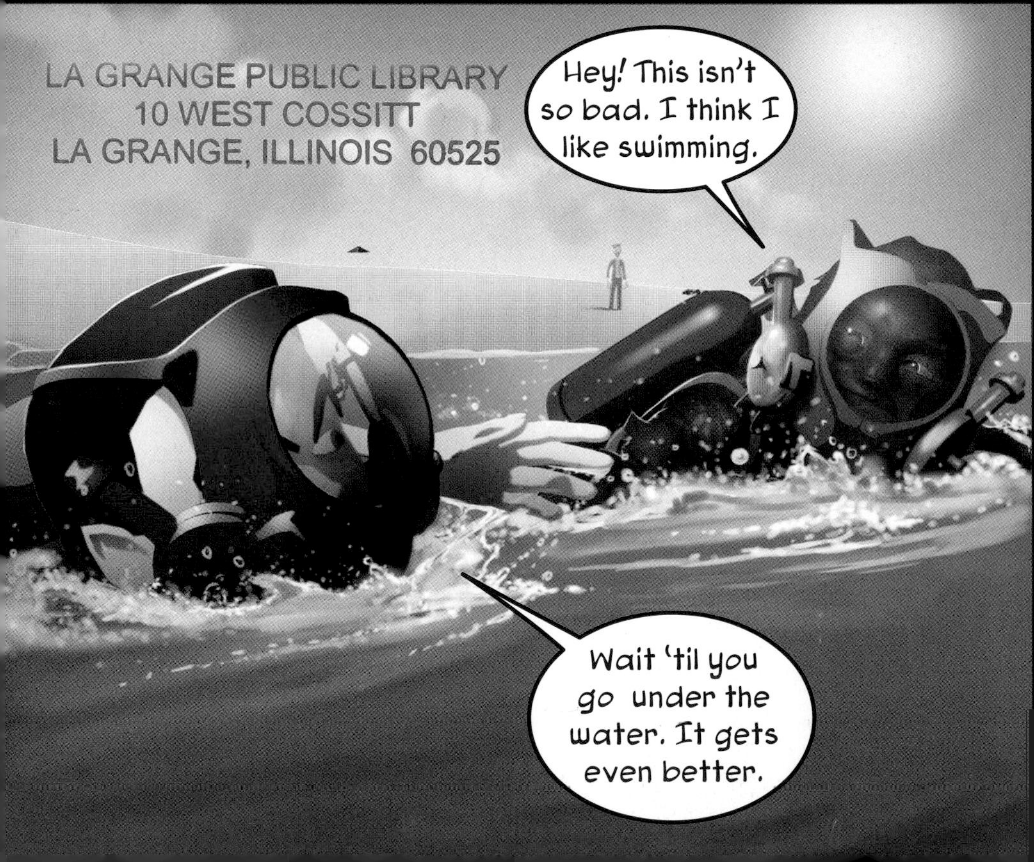
Hey! This isn't so bad. I think I like swimming.
Wait 'til you go under the water. It gets even better.

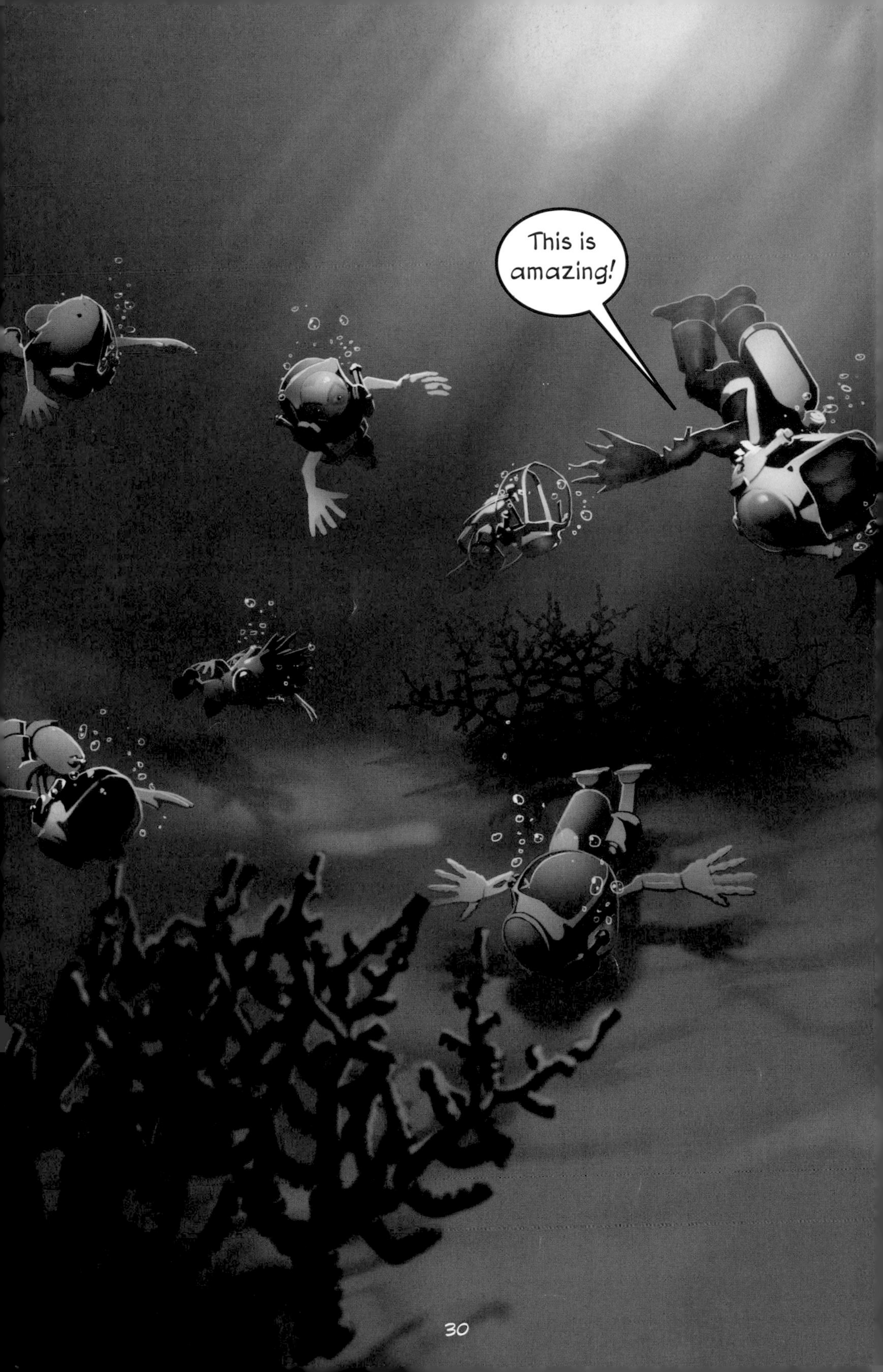
This is amazing!

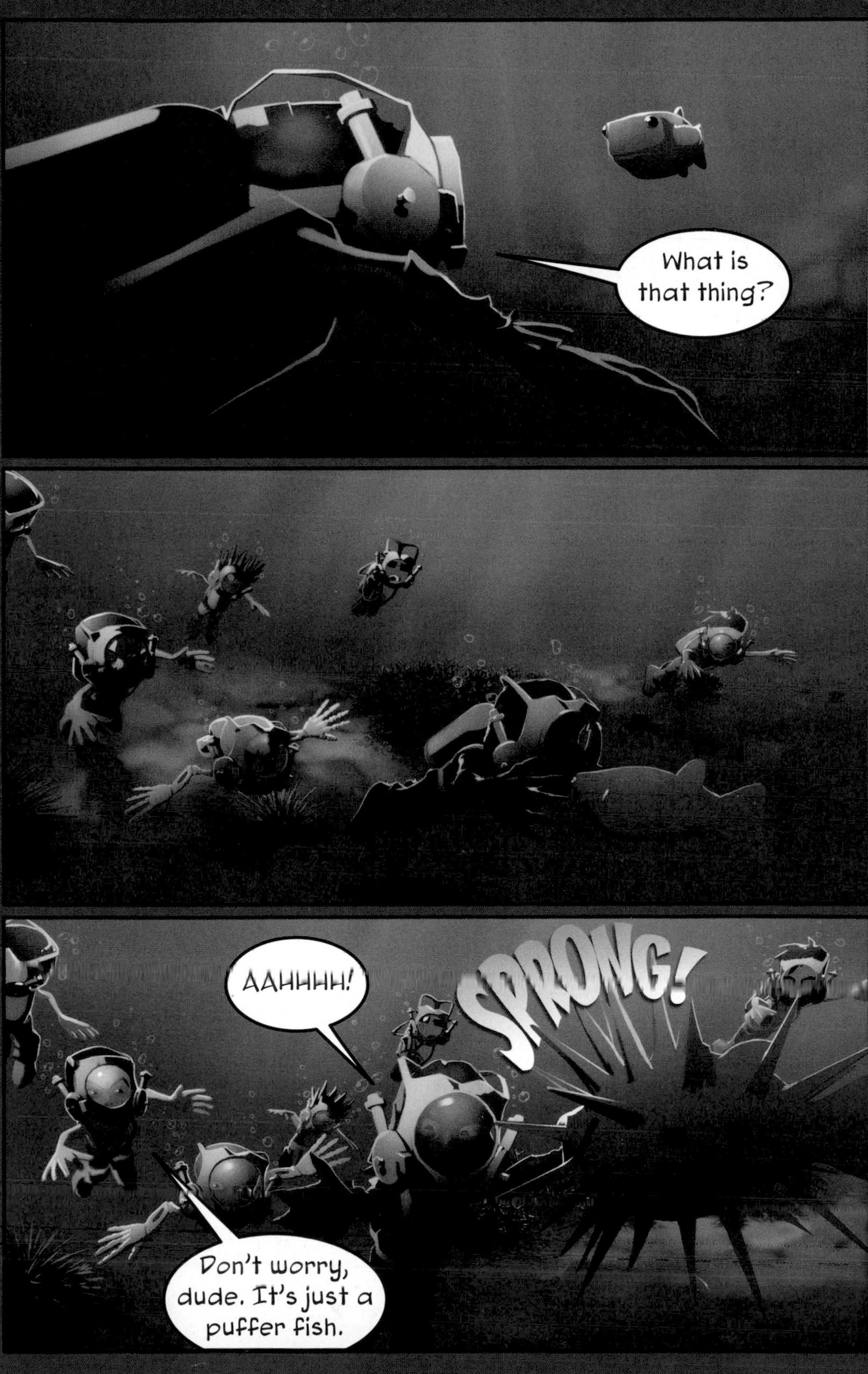
What is that thing?
AAHHHH!
SPRONG!
Don't worry, dude. It's just a puffer fish.

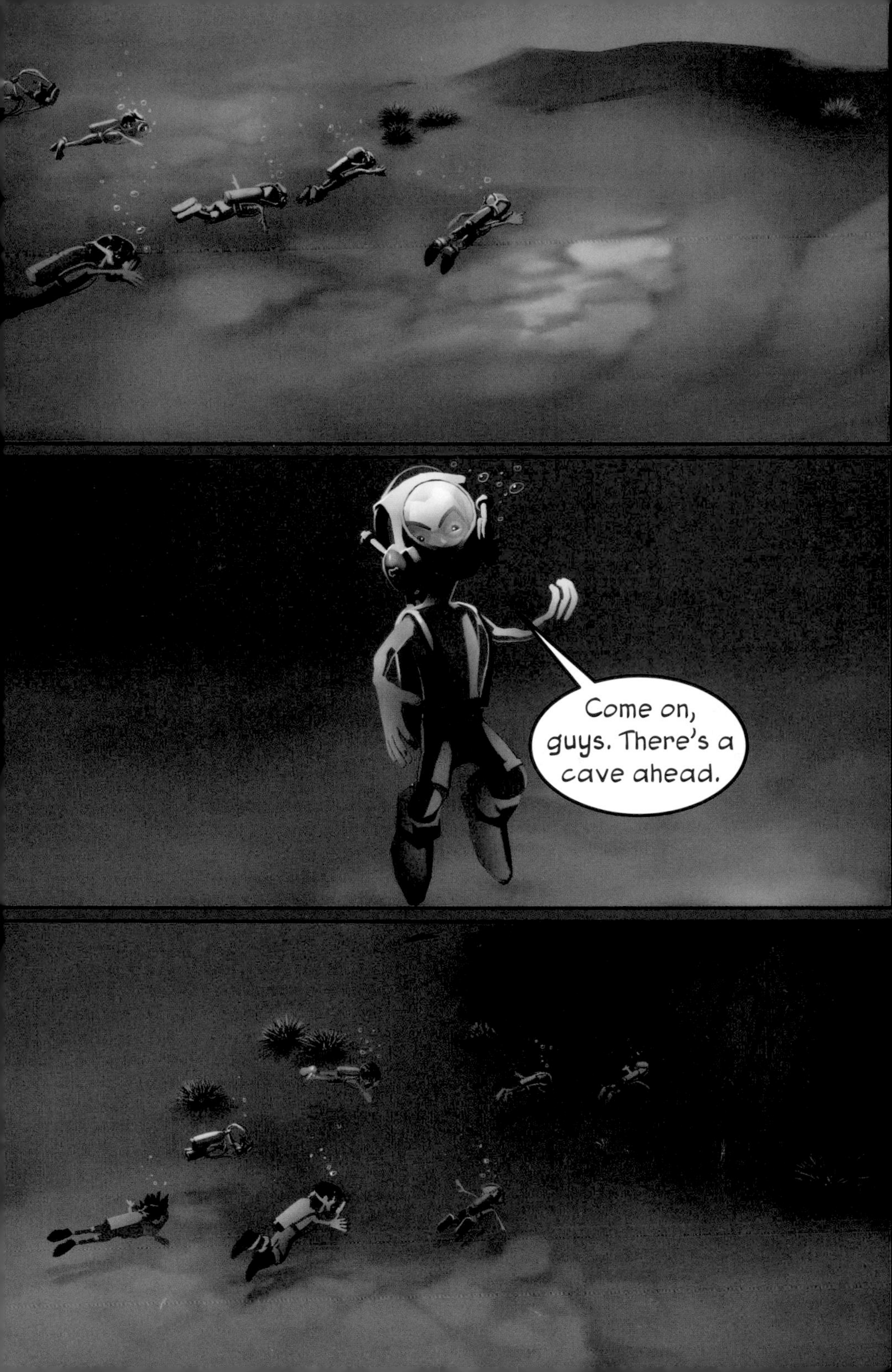
Come on, guys. There's a cave ahead.

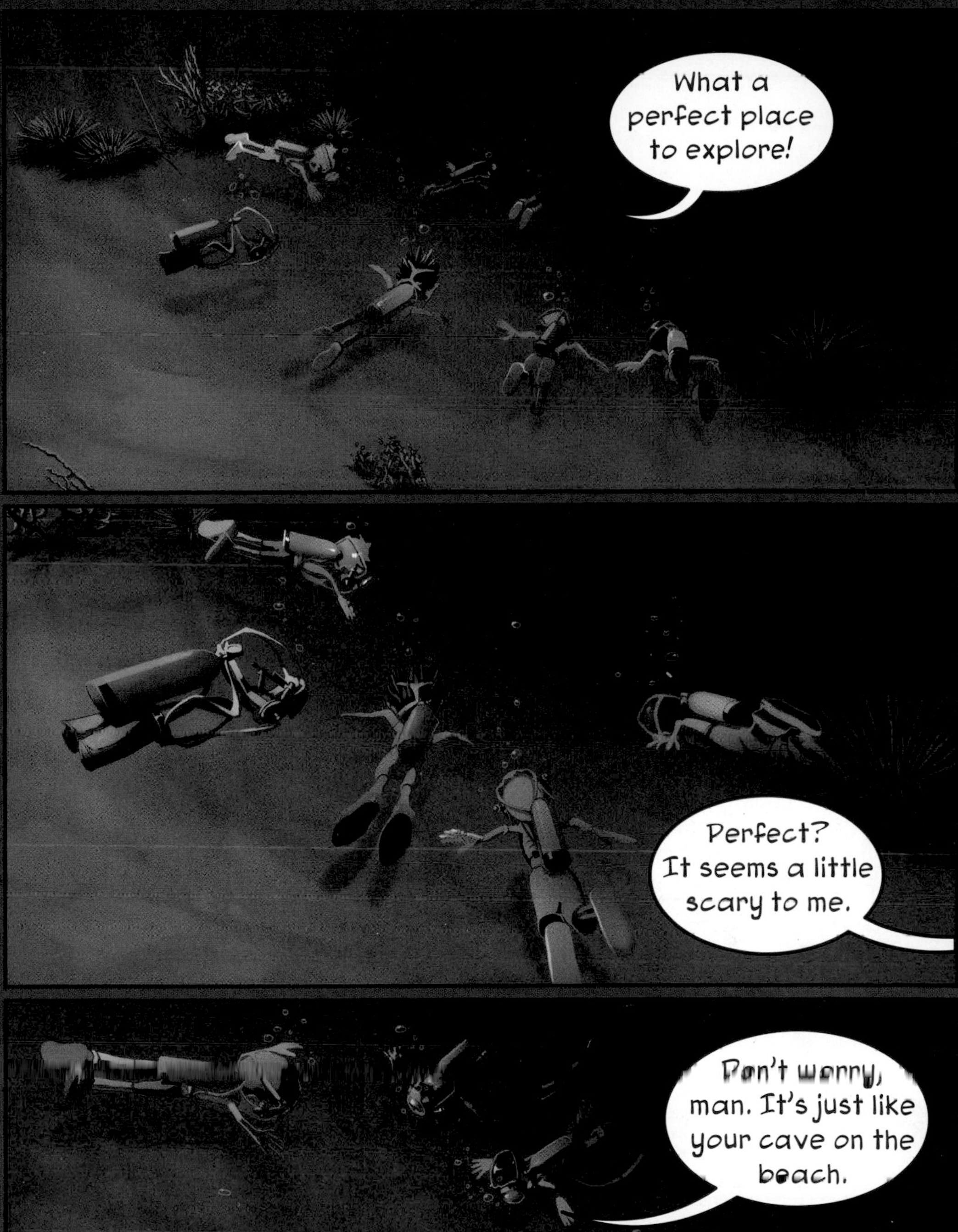
What a perfect place to explore!
Perfect? It seems a little scary to me.
Don't worry, man. It's just like your cave on the beach.

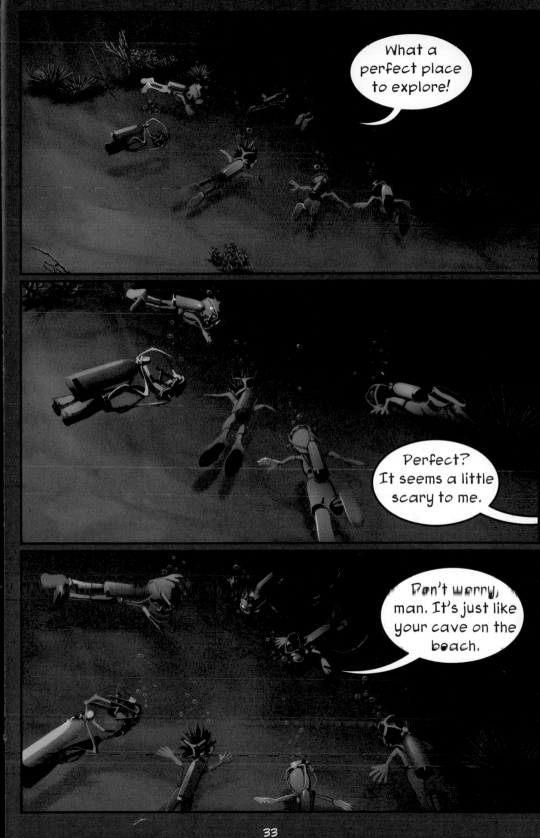

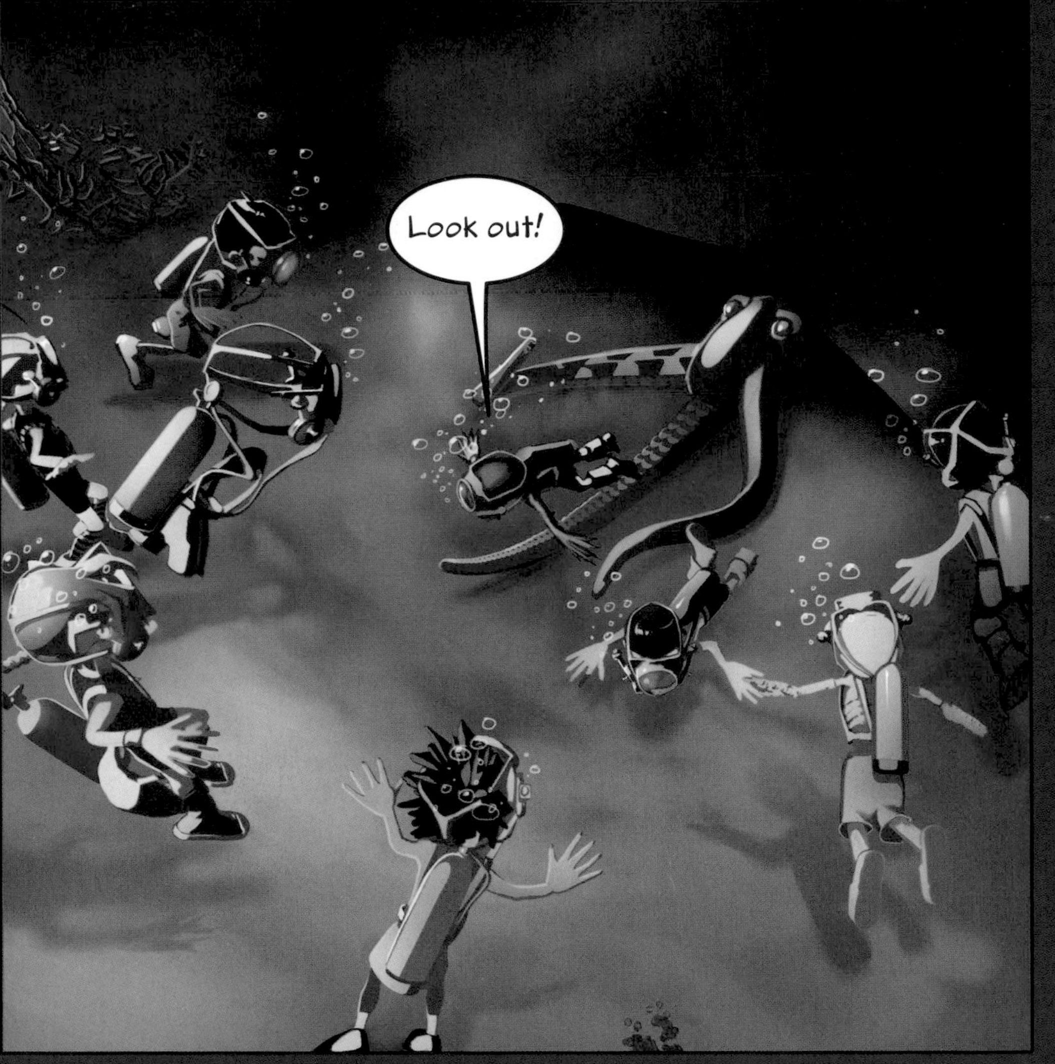
Look out!

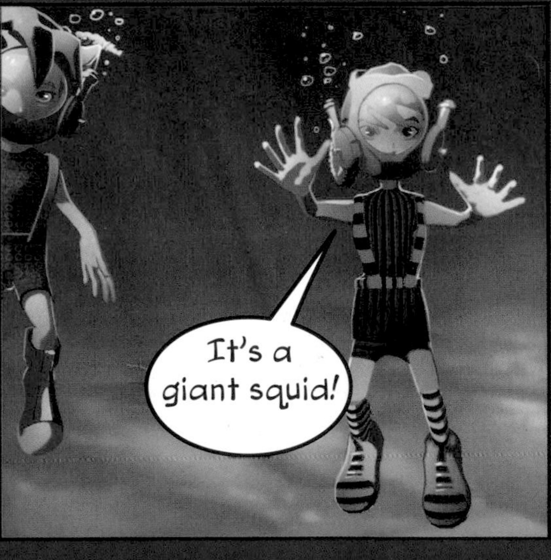
It's a giant squid!

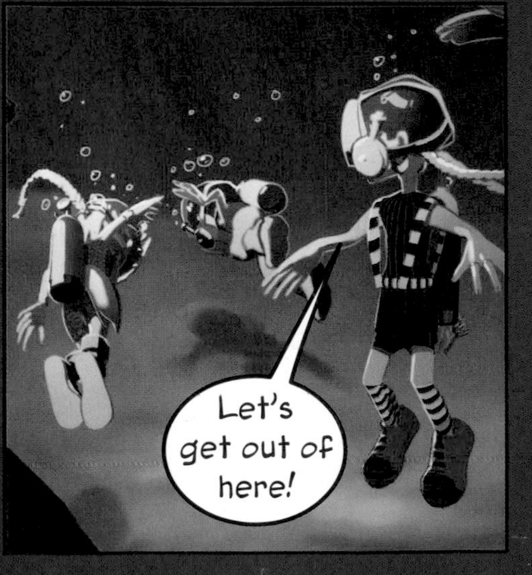
Let's get out of here!

Oh no!
He got us!

Help us,
Gil!

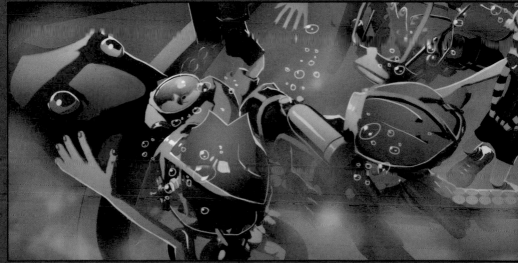

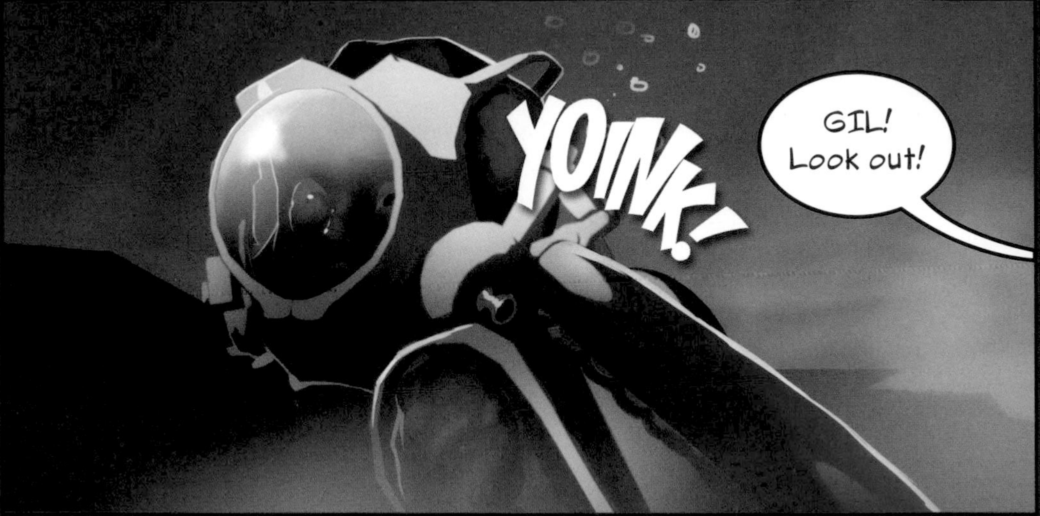
YOINK!
GIL! Look out!
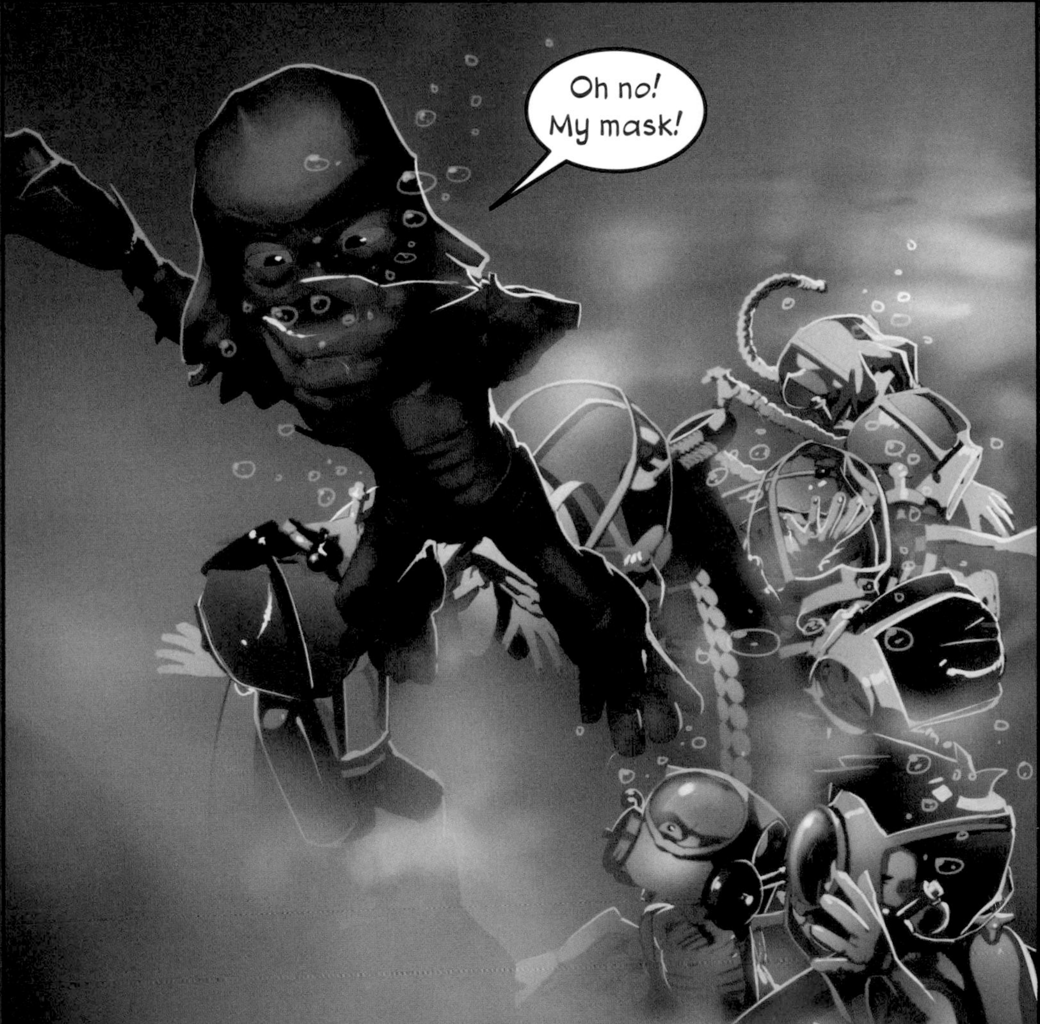
Oh no! My mask!

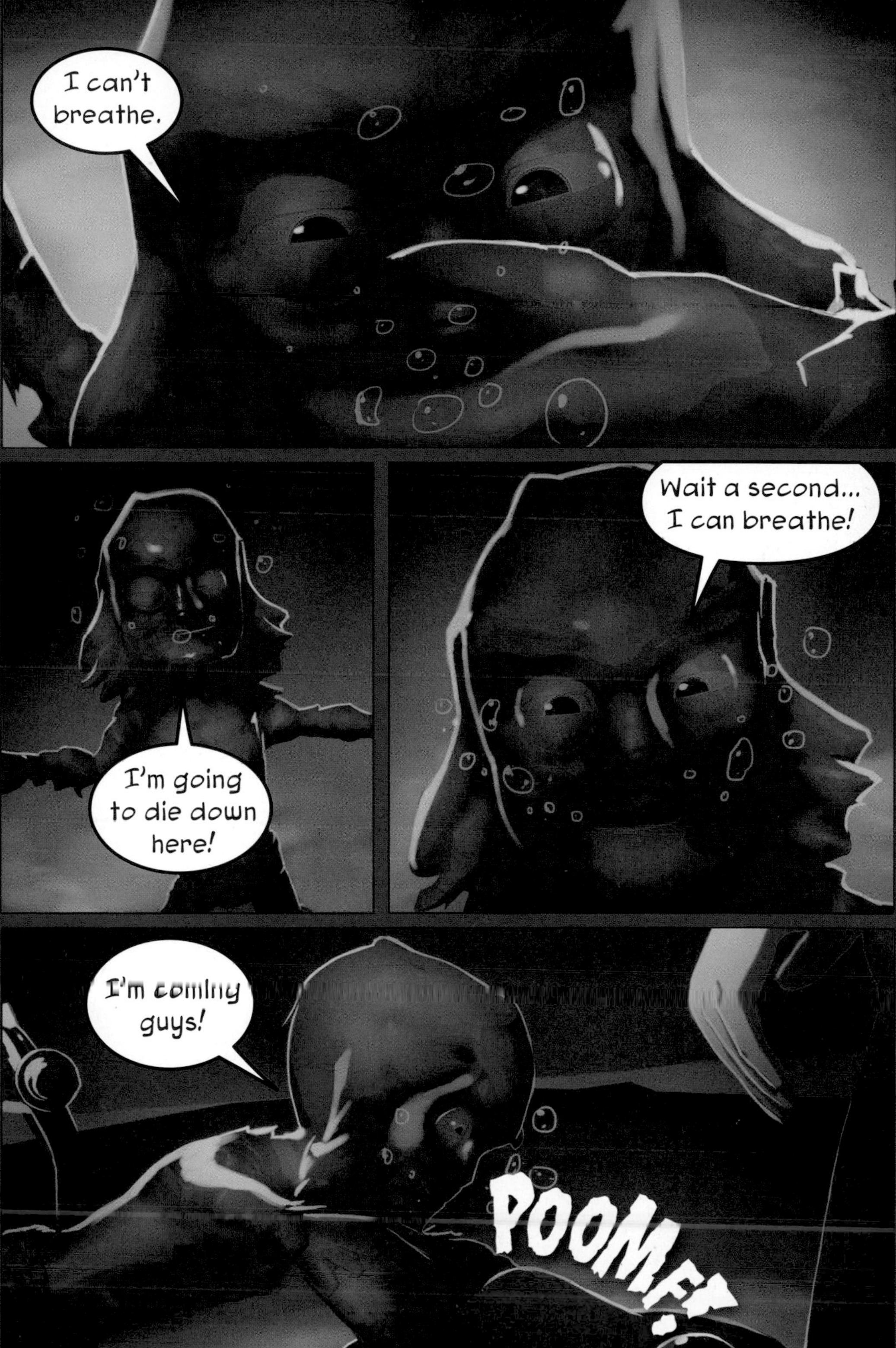
I can't breathe.
I'm going to die down here!
Wait a second... I can breathe!
I'm coming guys!
POOMF!

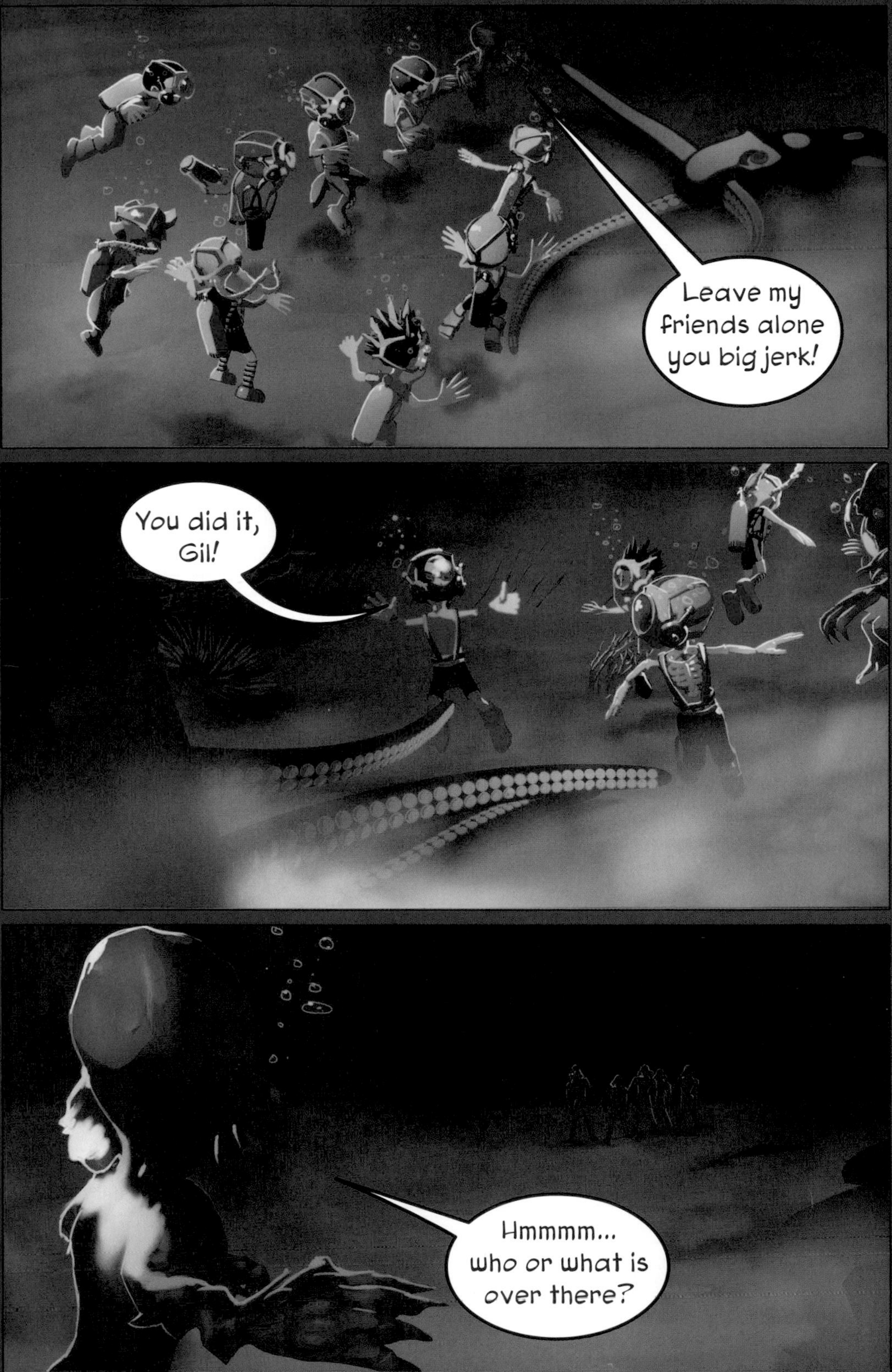
Leave my friends alone you big jerk!
You did it, Gil!
Hmmmm... who or what is over there?

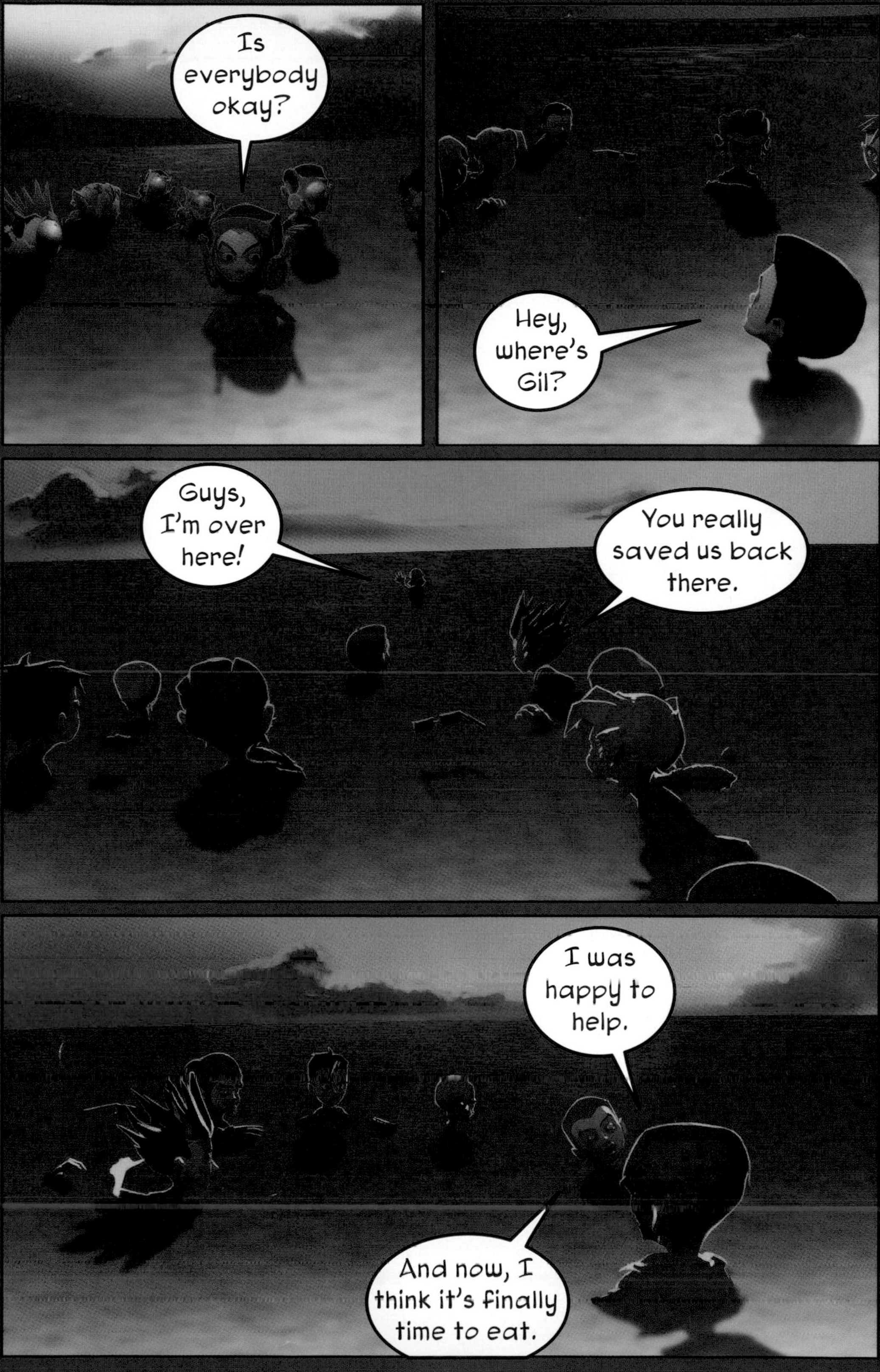
Is everybody okay?
Hey, where's Gil?
Guys, I'm over here!
You really saved us back there.
I was happy to help.
And now, I think it's finally time to eat.

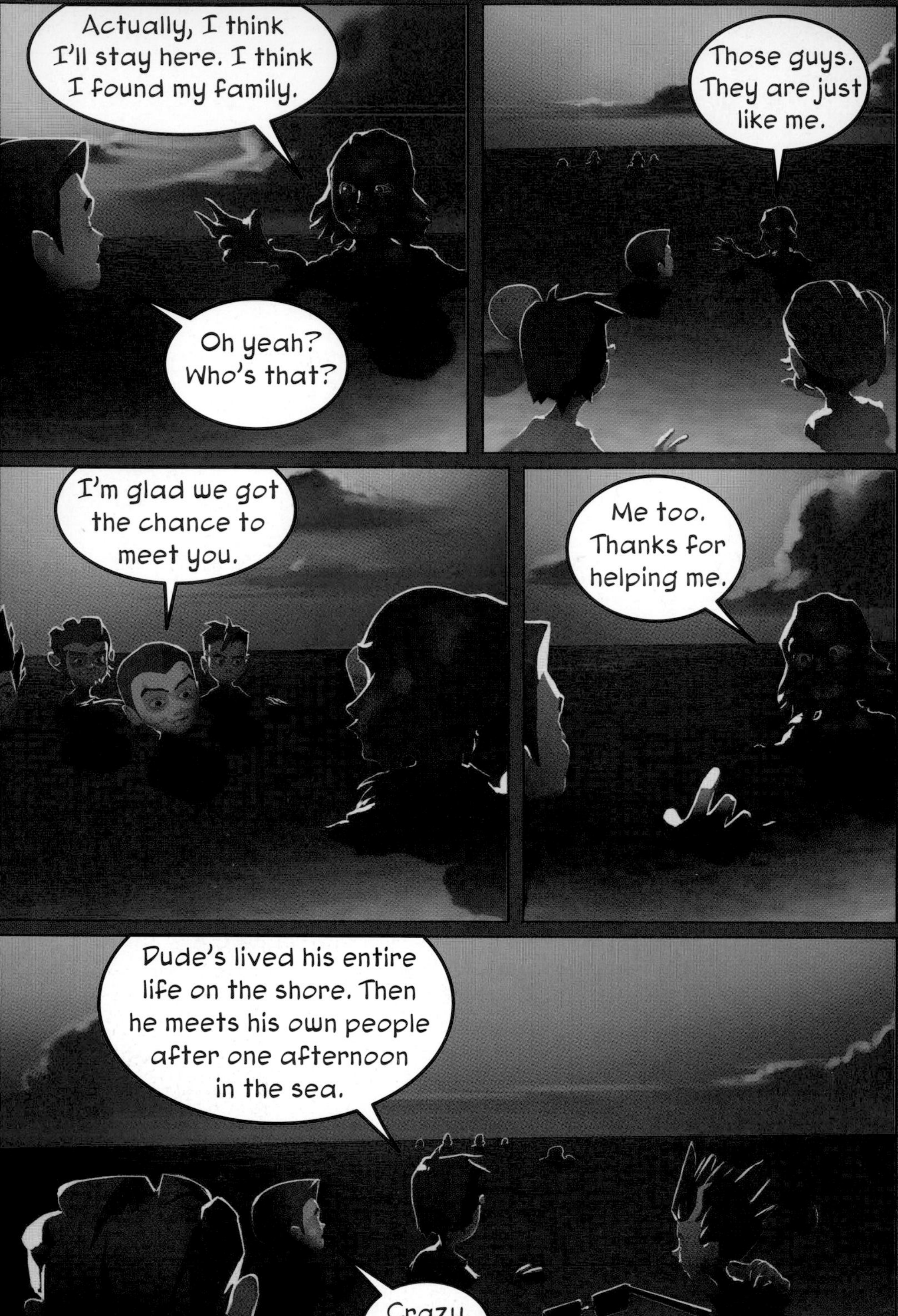
Actually, I think I'll stay here. I think I found my family.
Oh yeah? Who's that?
Those guys. They are just like me.
I'm glad we got the chance to meet you.
Me too. Thanks for helping me.
Dude's lived his entire life on the shore. Then he meets his own people after one afternoon in the sea.
Crazy, right?

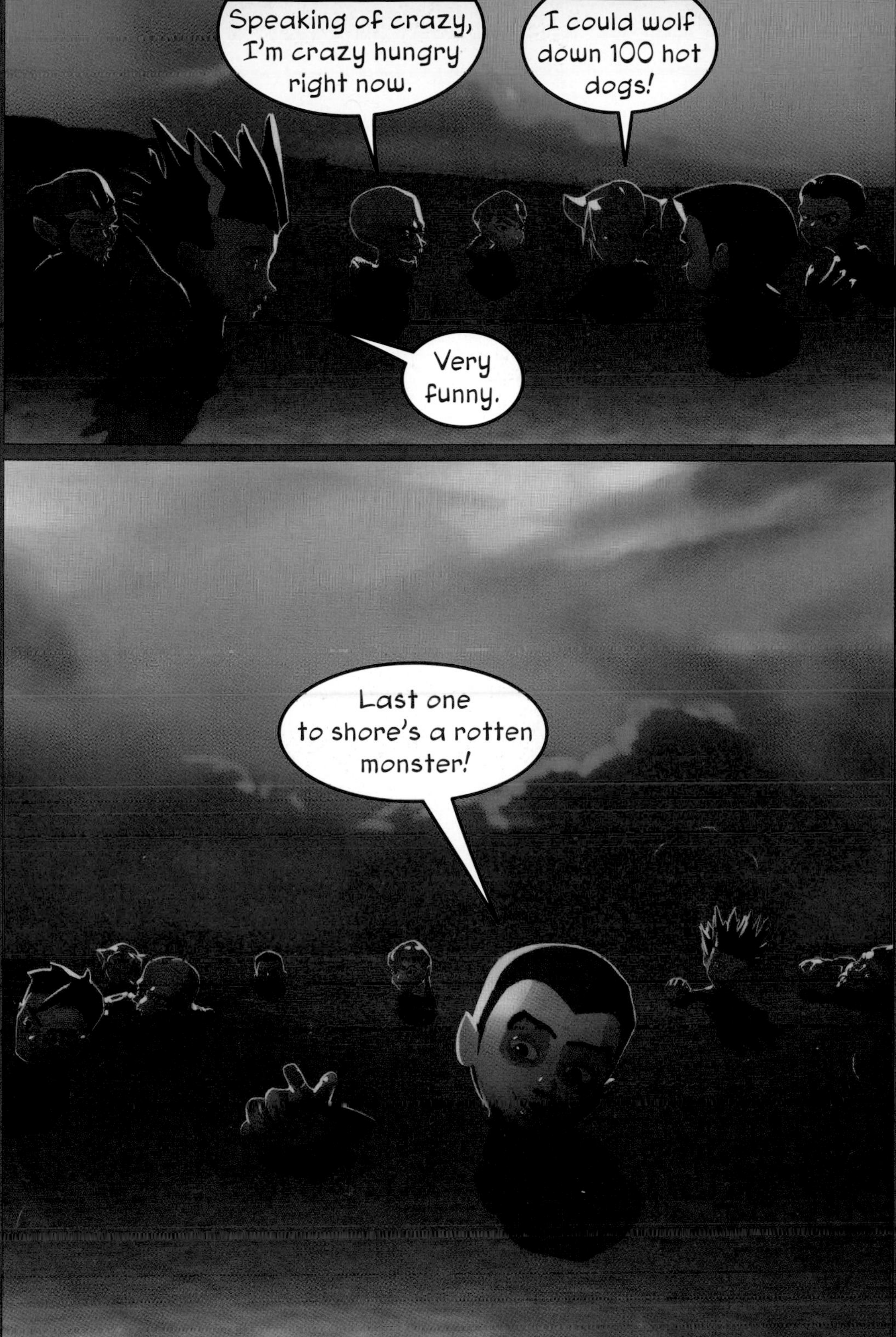
Speaking of crazy, I'm crazy hungry right now.
I could wolf down 100 hot dogs!
Very funny.
Last one to shore's a rotten monster!

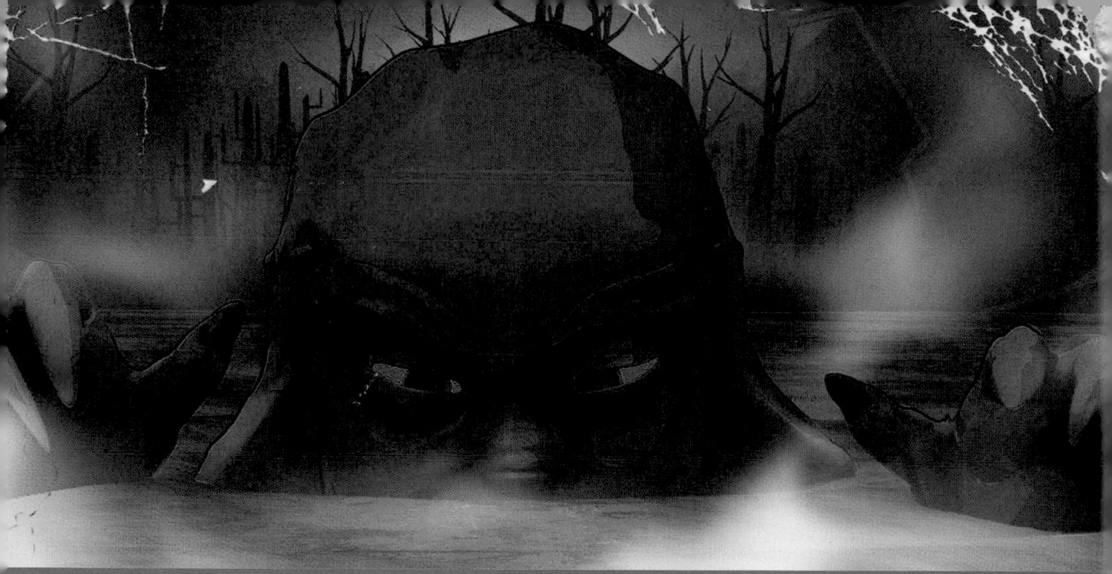

GET TO KNOW GIL!

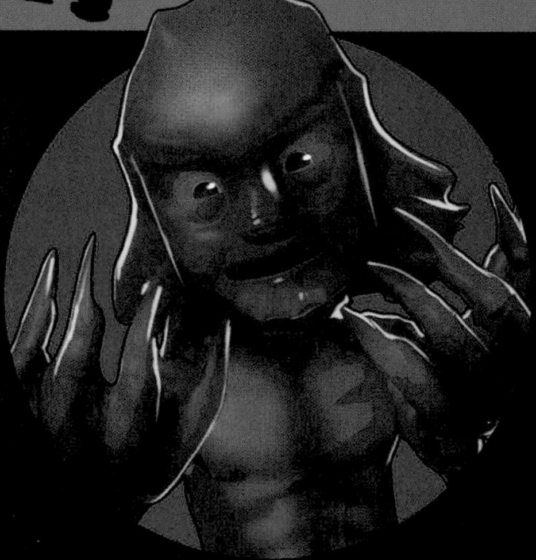

Full name: Gilliver Finn
Nicknames:
Gil, Greenie, Fishman
Hometown:
Beachville, California
Favorite Color: Green
Hobbies: Collecting seashells, reading, and spelunking

Biography

Shortly after Gil was born, the horror movie *Creature from the Black Lagoon* was released. This movie showed land and sea creatures as dangerous monsters. Gil's parents had no choice but to leave him on a deserted beach where he would be safe. Gil lived a lonely life until a small group of monsters saved him and reunited him with his family. Today, Gil runs a homeless shelter and hopes to find homes for every monster he meets. He is married and has five children.

GLOSSARY

intrigue (IN-TREEG)—a crafty, secret plot

mystery (MISS-tur-ee)—a story containing a puzzling crime that has to be solved

purpose (PUR-puhss)—deliberately rather than by accident

relaxation (ree-lak-SAY-shuhn)—to rest and take things easy

rotten (ROT-uhn)—gone bad

scuba gear (SKOO-buh GEER)—equipment used for breathing underwater while swimming

shore (SHOR)—the land along the edge of an ocean, river, or lake

DISCUSSION QUESTIONS

1. Gil was all alone on the beach until the monsters found him. How do you think he ended up by himself? What happened to his family?

2. Would you have helped Gil if you met him on the beach? Explain your answer.

3. Were you surprised by the ending of the book? Why or why not?

WRITING PROMPTS

1. When the monsters needed a break, they headed to the beach to relax. Write about something you like to do to relax.

2. Gil was scared of the water, but he conquered his fear. Write about a time when you did something you were scared of.

3. The monsters go scuba diving at the beach. Write a paragraph about your favorite thing to do at the beach.

award-winning comic book publisher with more than 150 graphic novels produced for Harper Collins, Simon & Schuster, Random House, Scholastic, and others.

Within a year, the company won many awards including the Shuster Award for Outstanding Publisher and the Moonbeam Award for top children's graphic novel. O'Reilly also won the Top 40 Under 40 award from the city of Vancouver and authored The Clockwork Girl for Top Graphic Novel at Book Expo America in 2007. Currently, O'Reilly is one of the most prolific independent comic book writers in Canada. While showing no signs of slowing down in comics, he now writes screenplays and adapts his creations for the big screen.

Mighty Mighty MONSTERS ADVENTURES

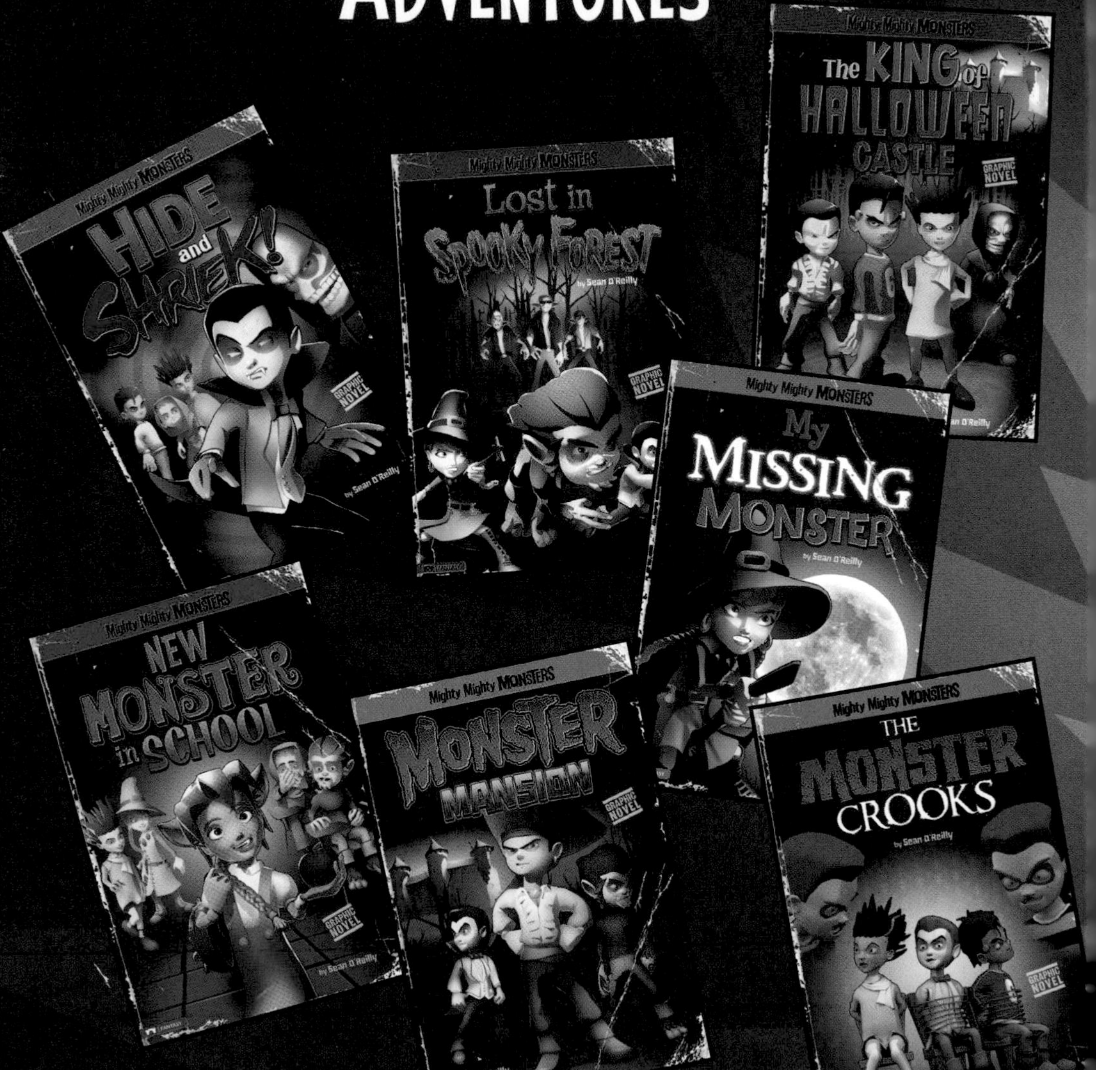
Mighty Mighty MONSTERS
HIDE and SHRIEK!
GRAPHIC NOVEL
by Sean O'Reilly
Mighty Mighty MONSTERS
Lost in Spooky Forest
by Sean O'Reilly
GRAPHIC NOVEL
Mighty Mighty MONSTERS
The KING of HALLOWEEN CASTLE
GRAPHIC NOVEL
Mighty Mighty MONSTERS
My MISSING MONSTER
by Sean O'Reilly
Mighty Mighty MONSTERS
NEW MONSTER in SCHOOL
GRAPHIC NOVEL
by Sean O'Reilly
Mighty Mighty MONSTERS
MONSTER MANSION
GRAPHIC NOVEL
by Sean O'Reilly
Mighty Mighty MONSTERS
THE MONSTER CROOKS
by Sean O'Reilly
GRAPHIC NOVEL

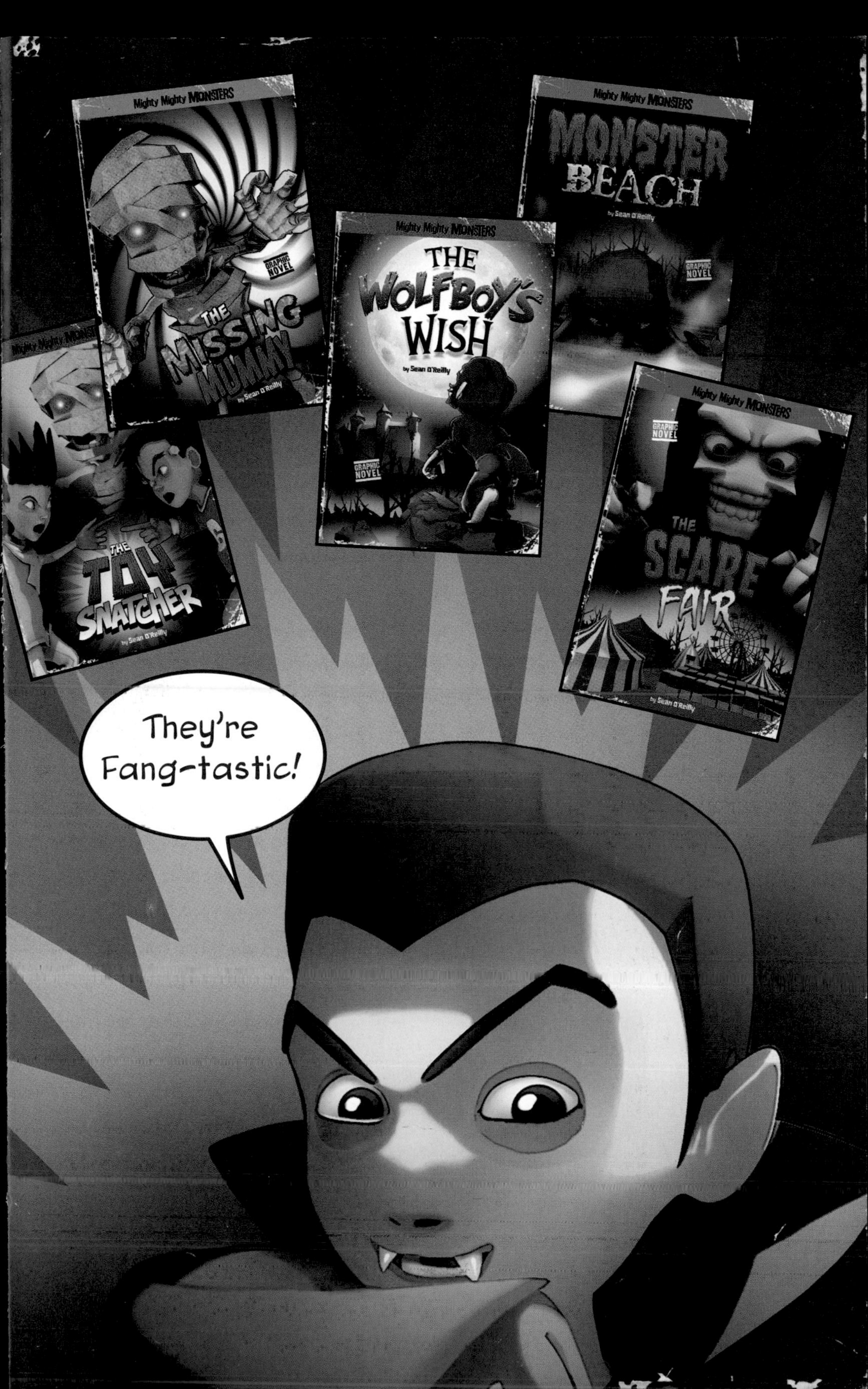
Mighty Mighty MONSTERS
THE MISSING MUMMY
by Sean O'Reilly
GRAPHIC NOVEL
Mighty Mighty MONSTERS
THE WOLFBOY'S WISH
by Sean O'Reilly
GRAPHIC NOVEL
Mighty Mighty MONSTERS
MONSTER BEACH
by Sean O'Reilly
GRAPHIC NOVEL
Mighty Mighty MONSTERS
THE TOY SNATCHER
by Sean O'Reilly
Mighty Mighty MONSTERS
GRAPHIC NOVEL
THE SCARE FAIR
by Sean O'Reilly
They're Fang-tastic!

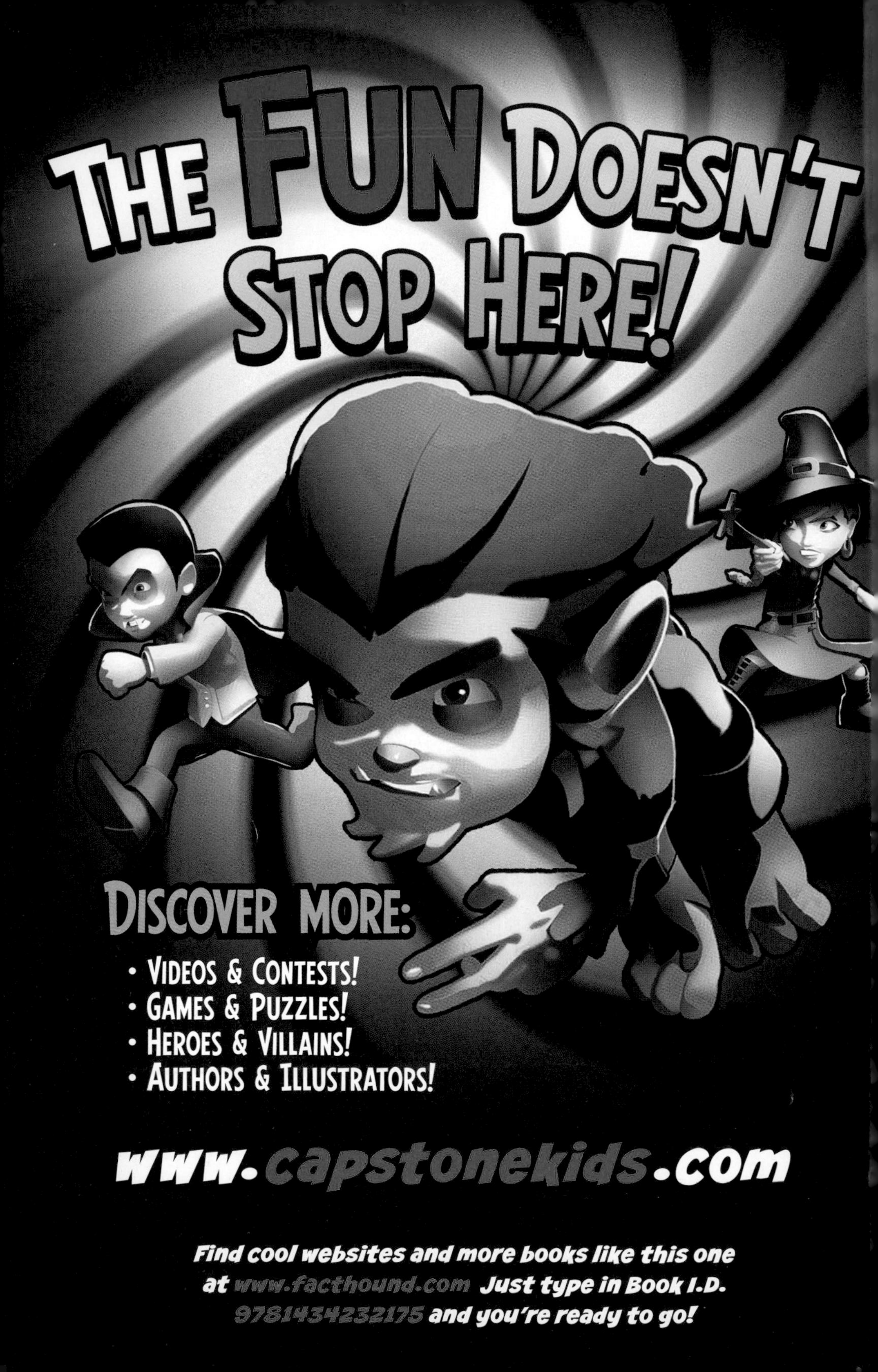
THE FUN DOESN'T STOP HERE!
DISCOVER MORE:
• VIDEOS & CONTESTS!
• GAMES & PUZZLES!
• HEROES & VILLAINS!
• AUTHORS & ILLUSTRATORS!
www.capstonekids.com
Find cool websites and more books like this one
at www.facthound.com Just type in Book I.D.
9781434232175 and you're ready to go!